Pamela Taylor

Second Son

Second Son Chronicles - Volume 1

To Rachel -
Best wishes always!

Pamela

Black Rose Writing | Texas

ISBN: 978-1-68433-063-8
PUBLISHED BY BLACK ROSE WRITING
www.blackrosewriting.com

Printed in the United States of America
Suggested Retail Price (SRP) $17.95

Second Son is printed in Book Antiqua

This series is dedicated to the hope that thoughtfulness, compassion, respect, and rational dialogue can triumph over bigotry, greed, mistrust, and self-righteousness to create a world that is truly a better place for all of humankind.

I'm particularly grateful to Linda Kirwin for her help and guidance. Though her project started as a beta read with critique, she quickly grasped what I was trying to do in this series and became a valued editorial consultant. Thanks also to the members of the DFW Writers Workshop who listened to readings and offered their food for thought. And a very special thank you to Jeffrey — himself a second son — who was my first reader and who encouraged me in the early days, when I was unsure if my vision was worth pursuing.

THE ROYAL FAMILY

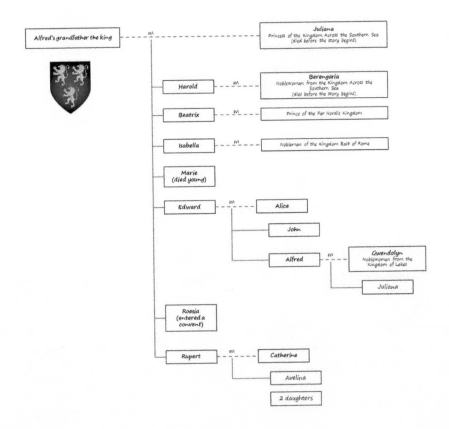

Alfred's grandfather the king — m — Juliana
Princess of the Kingdom Across the Southern Sea
(died before the story begins)

Harold — m — Berengaria
Noblewoman from the Kingdom Across the
Southern Sea
(dies before the story begins)

Beatrix — m — Prince of the Far Nordic Kingdom

Isabella — m — Nobleman of the Kingdom East of Rome

Marie
(died young)

Edward — m — Alice

John

Alfred — m — Gwendolyn
Noblewoman from the
Kingdom of Lakes

Juliana

Roesia
(entered a
convent)

Rupert — m — Catherine

Avelina

2 daughters

THE NOBILITY

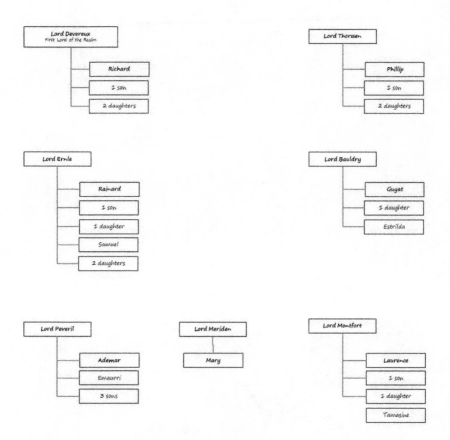

Lord Devereux
First Lord of the Realm
- Richard
- 1 son
- 2 daughters

Lord Thorssen
- Phillip
- 1 son
- 2 daughters

Lord Ernle
- Rainard
- 1 son
- 1 daughter
- Samuel
- 2 daughters

Lord Bauldry
- Guyat
- 1 daughter
- Estrilda

Lord Peveril
- Ademar
- Emaurri
- 3 sons

Lord Meriden
- Mary

Lord Montfort
- Laurence
- 1 son
- 1 daughter
- Tamasine

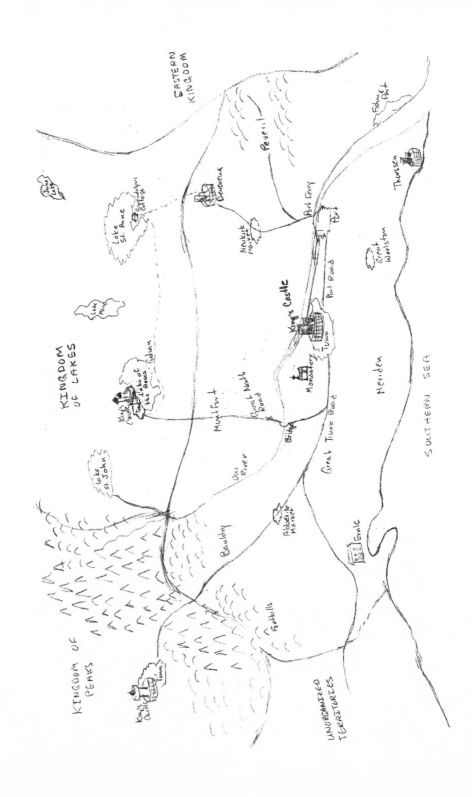

Second Son

Prologue

I have no expectations, for I am a second son and so my prospects are limited. Moreover, I am a second son of a second son, making me twice removed from the advantages of inheritance.

It is usual in our society that second sons are destined for the Church. There, a man who is ambitious and clever – and lucky – and also, perhaps, a bit ruthless – may rise to positions of comfort and power. Those of a more meek and selfless bent may be drawn to a life of service to others. But for many, it is a destiny of rules and deprivation and toil, and a life with little joy or satisfaction.

I am to be spared that fate, however, for our family is not usual. My grandfather is the king, and even second sons are important to ensuring the succession. So my destiny is to be always "in waiting" and to try to find a role for myself during a wait that could last my entire lifetime. In that, I am not unlike my father, though he is nearer the succession than I.

Our kingdom is at peace and prosperous, but that was not always so. In the dark times after the Romans left, it wasn't even a kingdom—just a patchwork of domains created when a strong leader could take and hold some land and subdue the people on it. My ancestors claimed the best parcels—including the inland harbor sheltered from sea storms, the monastery occupied by a small community of monks, and the remains of the Roman road leading westward—and built a fortress at the point where the river widens and becomes navigable by larger craft. Thus they controlled access to the sea and to any lands to the west. Such valuable territory came with a price, however, for they were often attacked by neighbors hoping to break out of their landlocked domains.

Around two hundred years ago, the lord of our domain decided that cooperation with his neighbors might be preferable to continually fighting them, so he put forth a bold proposal to form a unified kingdom . . . with himself as king, of course, since he was in possession of the most coveted territory. At first, he was met with derision, but the leader of the Devereux family soon recognized the advantages to be gained from unfettered access to the sea and decided to swear fealty to the new king. His agreement to put the interests of the kingdom ahead of his own came with conditions, however. The Devereux family would remain masters of their domain in perpetuity, and the head of the family would hold a title, a place in the king's court, and the right to advise the king on matters of governing, of waging war, and of levying taxes. Realizing that his ambition to consolidate and expand his power wouldn't be achieved without some sort of compromise, my ancestor agreed, and the fledgling kingdom was born.

It wasn't long before six other domain holders decided they would rather be part of this new arrangement than be at the mercy of a larger, stronger neighbor that now controlled not only access to the sea and the route west but also both banks of the river at the harbor and an important road north. One by one, they pledged their loyalty to the new king, and the kingdom as we know it today was formed. Today's hereditary lords are the direct descendants of those men who so long ago decided they were stronger together than apart, and Lord Devereux holds the special honor of First Lord of the Realm.

Over several generations, the leaders of the new kingdom had to fight to protect their borders and their interests until finally, in my grandfather's grandfather's reign, their strength and determination won a fragile peace and some tentative alliances were formed. My great-grandfather strengthened those alliances through marriages and trade; and though my grandfather has always maintained a strong fighting force, his reign has been one of peace and increasing prosperity.

He's used this fortunate state of affairs to spread literacy and new ideas among our people and is abetted in this endeavor by his great friend Abbot Francis. As a very young monk, Francis befriended the boy who would later be king, taught him Latin, and opened his eyes to the wealth of knowledge in the books that the monks collected from near and far — books that were once rare indeed, so many having been lost or destroyed during the dark times. My grandfather has followed in the monks' footsteps, collecting books wherever he can find them and assembling a great library that he allows everyone at court to use.

He encouraged me, from a very young age, to read and even spent time helping me with some of the more difficult texts. "There's nothing more valuable than knowledge, Alfred," he once told me. "Men can take your belongings, your lands, even your family . . . but no one can take what's in your mind. And even in the face of what might seem the worst catastrophe, you can use what's in your mind to rebuild. So fill your mind from these books. You'll never regret having done so."

The last thing I remember before the world went dark was watching my arrow find its mark, saving my uncle from almost certain death. And the look—seemingly of recognition—on my victim's face as he turned toward me in his final agony. And the distant thunder of hoof beats—a troop of knights rushing to our rescue—a rescue that may have come too late for me.

I regain my senses to find myself draped across the shoulders of a horse, its rider in the saddle behind me. I decide to keep my return to consciousness secret for the moment, in hope of learning something about my situation. What I can see from this position, without turning my head or betraying my wakefulness, is limited. We're not on an open track or main road. From the abundance of leaves and underbrush beneath the horse's feet, I deduce we're in some kind of wood. Presumably, the rider wishes to remain unseen and undiscovered. There's a gentle undulation to the land as we move forward. A sign, perhaps, that we're skirting the edge of low hills? There's no way to determine our direction of travel, as the shade blocks any indication of the position of the sun. I detect no other horses nearby and no sound beyond what's made by our own horse, so we must be traveling alone.

My head aches dreadfully from the blow, the pain made even worse by my position, which causes the blood to flow to my head. My hands and feet are bound and tied together beneath the horse's chest. Though this may only be a precaution to keep me from falling off should the rider need to move swiftly, it seems more likely an indication that the rider is my captor and not my savior. Deciding there's nothing more I can learn from where I am, I stir visibly and turn my head to try to look up at the rider.

"You wake at last. I was beginning to think I'd done more damage than what I intended." He says nothing more . . . just rides on in silence. I, too, remain silent, not wishing to give him any indication of fear or desperation.

The bones of the horse's withers press into my stomach and lower ribs as he walks – right, left, right, left – adding to my misery. After what seems like an eternity but is probably no more than a quarter of an hour, I ask, "Who are you? Where are we going?"

There's no reply. And there is now no doubt . . . this man is clearly my captor.

We ride on until the shade deepens even more, night beginning to fall. The sound of running water must be a stream nearby. We stop. He dismounts, slings me over his shoulder, and takes me to a tree. He seats me facing the tree, then releases and reties the bindings on my hands so that I'm hugging its trunk. He does the same with my feet. He has no intention that I should escape.

He unsaddles his horse, hobbles it, and sets it to forage for something to eat under the leaves. Then he disappears. Returning with a flask and a cup, he pours water into the cup and holds it for me to drink. I had no idea I was so thirsty, but the water is sweet and I gulp it down, hoping for more.

He retrieves a loaf of bread from his pack, tears off a chunk, and holds it for me to eat. Then he pours another cup of water. While he's pouring, I ask again, "Who are you?"

This time he answers. "I know who you are. That's all that matters." He holds the cup for me to drink. When I finish, he throws the saddle blanket across my back for warmth and wanders off to make his own bed.

I'm anything but comfortable. The trunk of the tree is substantial and the way I'm bound prevents any possibility of reclining, but the upright position has at least relieved some of the pounding in my head. I lean against the tree, not expecting to sleep, my mind intent on working out how to escape. I struggle to devise a way to loosen the ropes around my wrists, but the girth of the tree is such that neither hand can reach the knots on the other. Trying to fray the rope by sliding it up and down against the rough bark does nothing but chafe my forearms. Getting a hand down to an ankle to untie those knots proves equally futile. The increasing girth of the tree nearer the ground prevents sliding even one hand downward more than a few inches—not nearly enough to reach an ankle.

Soon, reason overcomes my desperation. Even if I were to succeed in getting myself free, where would I go in these woods in the dark with nothing but a waning moon? The deep leaves on the forest floor could be hiding all manner of hazards that might leave me injured and alone. Besides, all those leaves would make it impossible to move silently. Better, perhaps, to spend my time thinking about how to overwhelm my captor in daylight when he must inevitably untie me to proceed on whatever journey he has in mind. So I slump against the tree and start plotting how best to catch him unawares.

Exhaustion must have overtaken me, for the next thing I know, it's morning, and my captor is kicking me awake. He's saddled his horse and tethered it to a low branch. In his hands is a long length of rope with a noose tied at one end, which he slips over my head and tightens enough to be sure I know he means business. He unties my hands and rebinds them in front of me, then unties my feet and hoists me into a standing position. My muscles are stiff and I fear falling, but I will myself to stay upright and show no sign of weakness. Pointing into the woods, he says, "Go relieve yourself. But don't think you can run away. All I have to do is pull on this rope and the noose will tighten. You'll only succeed in hanging yourself."

I take my time attending to nature's call, willing him to be distracted by something – an animal scurrying through the leaves and brush – a nicker from his horse – anything that would give me even a momentary advantage. Eventually, I can dawdle no longer. As I turn to walk back, I grab the noose in my hands and start running toward him, hoping to close the distance before he can react. Without hesitation, he gathers up the slack in the rope and yanks hard, pinning my hands between the noose and my neck, leaving me gasping for breath. Then he tugs me toward him like a fish on a line.

"I warned you," he says, as he loosens the noose just enough to free my hands before readjusting it to its original tautness.

After rebinding my wrists behind my back, he unties his horse and mounts. It's clear I am to walk. "Let's go," he says. "Remember. You lag or try to run, I yank on the rope."

Walking in the leaves and brush with fallen twigs and branches takes all my concentration. At least our pace is measured and I don't have to run. We emerge from the woods at midday and stop at a stream. Binding me once again to a tree, my captor fills his flask in the stream then repeats the ritual of giving me bread and water – this time with a few morsels of cheese – before eating his own.

Then we're on our way again. We ford the stream and soon arrive at a track that leads gently downhill to what appears to be a main road, where we turn to the right. Watching the path of the sun through the afternoon, I know for certain that we're moving west, away from my home. My mind screams No! Escape! Run! In the opposite direction! But with my hands tied behind my back, the options are limited. I could fall and feign an injury then try to use my legs and feet to incapacitate my captor. But perhaps if I show a bit of cooperation, he'll tire of having to feed me and rebind my hands in front of me to make his own life easier. At least then, I'd have a chance to grab the lead rope or to use my bound hands like a club to fight him.

As the sun begins to lower in the sky, we arrive at a walled town with a fortress in the center. We pass through the gate unchallenged and go directly to the smithy. "We'll sleep in your stable tonight," my captor informs the blacksmith, using numerous hand gestures to indicate his meaning. We must be in a place where people don't speak our language. "In the morning, I'll have work for you. Have your fires ready by sunup." The blacksmith doesn't argue. He's either terrified or knows this man or is accustomed to the presence of outlaws and brigands.

I'm given bread and water and taken to the hay loft for the night. My hands are tied around one of the posts supporting the roof and my feet around another nearby. At least tonight I'm able to lie down in the hay to sleep, a great improvement over hugging a tree.

I'm kicked from the depths of sleep at what I judge to be dawn from the faint light rising from the smithy below. I'm untied and ordered down the ladder, my neck rope held firmly in the grip of my captor. It's then that I discover I am to be the object of the blacksmith's work this day. I'm bound to a chair by ropes tied firmly around my chest and across my lap. The blacksmith ties on his apron while his apprentice works the bellows to stoke the fires.

"Wrist shackles first," orders my captor, drawing with a stick in the dirt to indicate what he wants, since neither seems to have much of the other's language. "One side fixed, the other with a hasp so I can unlock it to bind his hands in front of him, behind, or around a pole or tree. The chain between them short—about half the length of a man's foot."

Despite knowing what's about to happen, I'm oddly fascinated by watching the blacksmith work. Four half-circlets of metal. A single loop of chain attached to two of them. A length of chain measured to my captor's specifications and affixed at each end to a half-circlet. A hinge and a hasp and one shackle is complete. As he approaches me with this hardware, the noose around my neck tightens. Even the slightest additional tug and the rough rope would start cutting into the skin of my neck. I've no choice but to submit.

The apprentice brings red-hot metal from the fire, and they use that to weld the remaining two circlets around one wrist. The shackle with the hinge is wrapped around my other wrist, a lock placed through the hasp, and the key handed to my captor. The pressure on my neck relaxes somewhat.

"Leg shackles next," comes the order, accompanied by more drawing in the dirt. "He should be able to walk but not run." The blacksmith returns to work.

About halfway through the making of the leg shackles, a group of some eight or ten armed and mounted men appears at the smithy. Their leader, apparently parroting a few words he's been given, addresses my captor. "Our lord want talk."

"Then he'll just have to come down here," my captor replies

insolently. "I've a prisoner to guard."

From the middle of the group, a voice says, "I rather thought you might say that," and those in front move aside to let this man pass through. He's heavily armed and sits his saddle with the authority of one who knows he's in charge. On his head is a small coronet. Clearly the local lord. He appears to be just a few years older than me and he speaks our language. "What business have you here?" he asks.

"What you see in front of you."

"And that is all?"

"Aye." It seems this is going to be the end of the exchange; then my captor turns to face the lord. "But maybe you could do something for me."

"I doubt it, but make your request."

"I need a message sent . . . to the king of the lands next to yours. Tell him I have something that belongs to him. Tell him I want a ransom. And every day that I don't get that ransom, I'll take his grandson farther and farther away, and the size of the ransom will get larger and larger."

"And why should I send such a message? This is no business of mine, and we have no disputes with our neighbors."

"No reason. Just thought I'd ask." And he turns his attention back to observing the blacksmith at work.

After a moment, the lord asks, "And what are your intentions once this . . . business . . . ," he speaks the word with distaste, "is finished?"

Without looking back at his questioner, my captor replies, "You've nothing to fear from me. I've no quarrel with you. We'll be on our way. Like I said . . . taking this man farther and farther away from his king."

"See that you're gone by sundown," says the lord, and he and his guards turn and ride away.

The business at the smithy takes most of the rest of the day. My ankles are shackled. Chains are fitted between the shackles on my wrists and those on my ankles – barely long enough that I can eat and drink if I bend my head down to my hands – intended, quite obviously, to prevent my being able to raise my hands above my head to attack my captor. Finally, the noose is replaced with a metal collar, to which a rope can be attached to keep me under control. My captivity is complete.

Obeying the lord, we pass out through the gates of the town before sundown, but camp for the night within sight of the walls. Once again, I'm tethered to a tree trunk, but this tree is small enough I can slide my arms down to the base of the trunk and get into a more or less prone position for sleeping. As my captor throws the saddle blanket over me, I speak for the first time today. "You're a fool, you know."

He says nothing.

"My king will pay no ransom. That's not his way." I have no intention of confirming to him my relationship to the king.

He turns and looks down at me. "I wouldn't be so sure about that. From what I hear, you're his favorite. If he's any sort of man, he'll pay to get you back."

Oh, how little you know, I think to myself. If you but knew what sort of man my grandfather is, you'd know he would never stoop to your game, no matter how much the results might break his heart.

In the morning, we take to the road again, my captor riding, me walking behind, led by my neck collar. The sense of urgency — of panic, almost — to get free returns. My mind tells me it's almost impossible now that I'm chained up with such limited freedom of movement. But that same mind says I *have* to try something. Around mid-morning, I start slowing my steps, gradually at first. My captor rides on, taking no notice of what's happening behind him. Nor does he take any notice when I slow further, and his steady forward pace eventually pulls me to the ground. I manage to turn as I fall so that I land on my back rather than flat on my face; but he plods on, dragging me across the hard, uneven road. Knowing that tearing my shirt or having the skin scraped off my back won't do me any good, I finally shout, "Alright! Stop! You win!" He slows his pace considerably but doesn't stop until I'm finally forced to beg, "Please!"

He stops his horse and turns in the saddle to look at me in what can only be described as amusement. "Walk or be dragged. I care not which." As I struggle to get back to my feet, the expression on his face turns into a smirk.

"Who *are* you?" I ask again.

Predictably, there's no response. But I resolve to ask him every day in the hope he'll eventually tire of the game and at least tell me his name. Even that would be some small comfort as I try to make sense of why he's doing this.

I realize I need to keep track of time and place if ever I should break free and need to find my way home. This is my third morning in captivity. The attack occurred on Sunday. Today is Wednesday. We're traveling west on a road that appears to have had much wagon traffic on it. I look for landmarks as we travel but see nothing of note. No wide flowing rivers. No distinctive hills or peaks to use as guides. So far, we've not come upon another town or village. I occupy my mind by writing an imaginary letter to Gwen, my wife. I tell her of my love and how much I miss her. I tell her that I'm traveling and describe the landscape, but omit the circumstances of that travel.

By now I know that my only hope of escape is for someone in a town or village – or someone we meet on the road – to challenge my captor with sufficient strength and conviction to set me free. How long will it be before that someone appears?

We continue to wander farther and farther westward, each day more or less the same as its predecessor. I'm kicked awake by my captor as the sun is rising. Every morning, I repeat my question, "Who are you?" occasionally adding, "Where are you taking me?" I've yet to be rewarded with a reply.

Somehow we always find a stream – even a small one – for our midday stop. It seems as if my captor knows this landscape. A cup of water, a small chunk of bread, a few bites of cheese . . . not a lot to sustain a man. At least now I can eat and drink for myself. In the afternoon, we plod on. My captor makes no effort to accelerate the pace beyond what a man can comfortably walk. He seems in no hurry to reach whatever destination he has in mind. At night, we camp in the open, always somewhere there's a substantial tree. I'm becoming adept at sleeping tied to a tree. In truth, it's not difficult after walking all day with very little food.

The days turn into weeks. We wander, seemingly aimlessly, often taking tracks off the main road. Now and again we find shelter for the night in a shed or a barn. Sometimes we find a small village. Sometimes we find another track that takes us back to the main road. More often, we retrace our steps.

Occasionally, we pass in the vicinity of a town. At each town, my captor leaves me tied to a tree well out of sight of the road, making sure I can't escape. For some reason, he seems to want to avoid my being seen by anyone. My hopes of rescue fall farther each time this happens. Even if he just left me there for someone to find me . . . But each time he returns with more bread and cheese and some grain for his horse. I know not and care not if he buys it or steals it, for it's the only thing that's keeping me alive. Neither do I know if he's repeated to whoever is in charge there his request to send a message to my grandfather. I can only assume he's received no answer, for we keep traveling west.

I try to burn the image of each town and fortress into my mind, but they're all so very similar, it's difficult to find any distinction. I've decided we must be traveling in the Unorganized Territories, a largely feudal society on the southwestern border of our kingdom where individual lords govern the lands within a day's ride of their stronghold. There's been no unrest along that border for many decades; but we know that the lords in the western-most reaches of the Territories are more bellicose, often skirmishing among themselves. From time to time, people from the Territories make their way across our border. It's not a large migration. It isn't easy for people in a serf-like state to muster the will to leave family or to succeed in getting away and making the journey. But it's been our practice throughout my grandfather's reign to accept those who make it across. Abbot Francis established a small monastery near the border village where we can provide the basic essentials for new arrivals for a short time. They usually arrive fearful and hungry without a really good idea of how they're going to make new life. For the most part, the eastern lords in the Territories turn a blind eye to this migration. From time to time, they'll capture a group before they reach us, but this seems more a token effort to remind their people who's in charge than any concerted attempt at prevention. Never in living memory has there been a hostile incursion across the border.

· · · · ·

I've given up trying to keep track of the days, having no easy way to record their passage. I've decided it's easier to keep track of the moon. One full moon has passed, and the moon is now waxing full for the second time since I was taken. I've lost weight as a result of the constant walking and dearth of food. My clothes hang looser on my frame, and I've had to hitch up my trousers to keep them from falling around my knees.

This road seems well traveled, yet we never encounter travelers. Is there something about the season of the year that makes people in these lands retreat to the safety of hearth and home, not to venture abroad again until the return of spring? Or are our diversions down tracks that go nowhere merely my captor's way of avoiding the time or place where he knows there'll be people about who might help me escape? His reluctance to take me with him into a town suggests the latter.

I still work to keep my mind occupied. I've tried to remember every poem I ever read. Some I remember well and can recite to myself. Others I remember only partially and occupy myself making up the parts that have vanished from my memory. I try to reconstruct from my readings the history of the Roman occupation of this land. I imagine sending a secret message to my grandfather and try to keep track of both the cipher and the coded message in my head. This is harder than I had thought it would be. Every third day, I write an imaginary letter to Gwen. This is getting more and more difficult because there is so little news to share with her.

The days are rapidly getting shorter and colder. At night, we must have a fire for warmth. The saddle blanket that my captor tosses over me for sleep can't keep out the cold. I wake each morning chilled to the bone, despite trying to use for warmth whatever leaves or brush I can gather round me with my limited range of movement. We've been lucky not to encounter an early winter storm.

Today, at mid-afternoon, we come upon a track that leads south from the main road. My captor turns to follow the track. I sense that we're descending ever so slightly and guess that we're moving closer to the sea. When we camp that night, he seems suddenly voluble. "Your grandfather should have my message by now."

"I'm afraid you're going to be disappointed by my king's reaction." I steadfastly refuse to admit to my identity.

"We'll just have to wait and see, won't we? It may be you who's surprised."

The next day, as the sun is lowering in the west, I see a small fortress compound directly ahead on our track. My captor quickens our pace slightly, apparently intent on reaching the compound by dark. We pass through the gate and are immediately challenged by a sentry. "I would speak to Lord Owen," my captor replies. So he knows the castellan, at least by name.

The sentry gestures for us to follow. We're led to the inner yard and to a building that appears to be the great hall. My captor dismounts, tethers his horse, and gives a tug on my rope, indicating I should follow. The sentry opens the door onto a noisy hall where men are eating at tables and a single individual occupies a table on a raised platform. As we enter, the noise immediately subsides, and all eyes turn toward us.

The man on the platform stands and smiles broadly. "Ralf, you old renegade. Come in . . . welcome!" and beckons us toward him. At last my captor has a name! "So what's this you've got here?" asks the man who, presumably, is Owen. He looks me up and down. He, too, has some of our language. Something they've cultivated in order to deal with Ralf? It seems he's spent time here before.

"With any luck, my fortune," replies Ralf. "Do you have somewhere safe I can put him?"

"Sentry," shouts Owen. "Put the prisoner in a cell in the lockup. Throw some blankets in so he doesn't freeze to death and give him some soup. He's too scrawny, Ralf," he adds jovially. "You need to fatten him up if you intend to get good money for him."

"Feed him if you like. I care not," says Ralf.

The sentry leads me away to a tower and up a circular flight of steps on the outer wall, shoves me into a small room at the top of the stairs, shuts the door, and disappears. I inspect my surroundings as best I can in the low light. There's a hard ledge apparently intended to serve as a bed. High in the outer wall are two small windows to let in a modicum of light and air but placed so as to be unreachable by any occupant of the room, let alone one trussed up as I am. As a prison cell, it's not the worst I've heard of. There's one rickety chair and a small table with uneven legs that rocks no matter how or where you position it.

At length, the sentry returns, accompanied by a kitchen maid carrying a tray. He throws some heavy blankets onto the ledge-bed and takes my rope close to the collar to prevent any movement. The kitchen maid puts the tray on the table and runs out. The sentry releases my rope and makes his exit. I hear the key turn in the lock.

I sit at the table and examine the contents of the tray. There's a small bowl containing some sort of broth with a few tiny bits of meat and some cabbage floating in it . . . a hunk of bread, slightly larger than what Ralf has been giving me . . . and a cup of water. I bring the bowl to my mouth and taste the soup. It's warm, and after all this time, it seems like the tastiest meal I've ever eaten. I'm tempted to gulp it down but know that my stomach is no longer accustomed to such things. So I begin slowly by tearing off morsels of bread and soaking them in the broth before eating them. When I'm convinced my stomach isn't going to revolt, I proceed to drink the remainder of the soup, savoring its warmth and chewing on the bits of meat until there's nothing left to chew. Finishing my bread, I bring the cup to my lips, but the water smells foul, so I set it back down without drinking.

I walk over to the ledge-bed and sort out the blankets. One I fold as a sort of mattress, to cushion the hardness and cold of the stone. I lie on my makeshift mattress and pull the other two blankets over me. Warm food, shelter, and warm blankets. Despite its being a prison, this is as close to civilization as I've been for many long weeks.

In the morning, I discover a bucket beside the door. It smells foul so is apparently intended for relieving myself. In the middle of the morning, a guard appears with a scullery maid. She takes the bucket, disappears for a moment, and returns it empty. The guard and scullery maid leave, and the key turns in the lock.

At midday, a guard passes a cup of water through the small barred window in the door. I hold it to my nose and once again detect a foulness. "Have you no fresh water?" I ask him.

"Is fresh," he replies. "Near sea. Taste like seawater. Will not kill ye. I drink." He gestures by holding his nose and pretending to drink from a cup.

"Perhaps," I answer and set the offensive cup on the table.

For three days, I see no one but the guards and the maids. A cup of water appears each midday. My supper each evening is a repeat of what I was given the first night.

On the fourth day, my midday water is delivered by Ralf himself. The guard opens the door, and Ralf enters bearing two cups of water. He sets both on the table and plops himself onto the chair. I fear it might break from the rough treatment he's giving it. He takes one of the cups, pinches his nose between his fingers, and gulps it down.

"You drink that stuff?" I ask.

"Aye," he replies. "When there's no ale about. It's wretched, but a man's got to drink. And it hasn't killed me or anyone here yet."

I take the other cup, sniff its contents, and grimace. He roars with laughter and reaches out to turn the cup up so that I'm forced to either drink or let it all run down and soak my clothes.

"Owen wants me to sell you to him," he says. "He'd put you to work in his fishing fleet . . . always needs extra men for that, what with boats getting lost in storms and men getting injured or maimed handling the boats or the nets. But I think I can get more for you in ransom than Owen would ever be willing to pay. What say you?"

I say nothing.

"I'm leaving you here for a few days," he continues. "Owen needs my help. The neighboring lord's been allowing his people to poach deer on Owen's lands. He wants me to help catch the culprits and then lead a raid on his neighbor." From this, I deduce that we must be in the western Territories, where the lords are always squabbling.

"You'll not be going anywhere. You'll be here when I get back . . . and maybe my ransom will be, too." He picks up one of the cups, tosses it in the air and catches it, and laughs at me again. Then he yells, "Guard!" And with that, he's gone. The key turns in the lock.

My daily routine is constant and predictable. My wrists are raw from the shackles, and I have sores around my neck from the collar. My hair and beard are long and ragged. My boots haven't been off since the shackles were affixed so I can only imagine the condition of my feet. I still have all the feeling in them and can wriggle my toes, so I take this as a good sign. My finger nails had gotten as long as a woman's so I've been chewing and tearing to trim them. The result is ragged and rough, but something of an improvement. No doubt when my boots finally come off, I'll have toenails the length of swords. The soles of my boots are starting to show signs of wear. I try to remain optimistic that they were sturdy to begin with and won't develop holes.

One night, the kitchen maid reaches into her pocket after placing my tray on the table. She hands me a small pot and points first to the pot and then to my wounds. I infer that the contents must be some sort of salve. I take it gratefully, but say nothing, knowing she's doing something that might not be approved.

The salve is wonderfully soothing. After several days, I'm convinced that it's actually effecting some healing. When the pot is empty, I leave it on my supper tray and am pleased to find a fresh pot beside my soup bowl the following night.

No one seems willing to take pity on me and set me free. Owen must have left orders that I'm to be held at all cost. I've no choice, however, but to test their resolve. One morning, while the scullery maid is going about her business, I try to rush past the guard. He slams me back so hard that I'd have cracked my head open on the stone floor if the rickety table hadn't broken my fall. Despite the extra nourishment from the broth, I'm fed only once a day, so I've recovered neither weight nor strength, and I'm forced to admit how foolhardy tangling with a guard would be.

Boring as it is, I make myself walk around my cell for at least an hour each day, knowing that if I let my muscles atrophy, I'll be unable to walk when we resume our journey. That it will resume, I'm certain, for I know there will be no ransom. My only other prospect is being sold to Owen. But I'm convinced Ralf is sufficiently venal and vindictive to continue moving me farther and farther from home as a point of honor and hoping to increase his expected ransom. I try to exercise my arms as well, but this is more difficult because of the limitations on movement that my chains create.

Some days I can hear a howling winter wind through my tiny windows. On such days there's nothing for it but to wrap myself in blankets and exercise more for warmth. Twice I thought I observed snow falling, but neither time did it last long. Perhaps it was just my imagination.

As Ralf's "few days" turn into seemingly endless weeks, there's nothing left for me to do but contemplate how I came to be in this predicament. It all began, I think, in the year of my thirteenth birthday.

It was the year in which I had to interrupt my schooling to learn the skills of tournament and battle required of the sons of a noble house. Though this is an important coming-of-age milestone for lads of my station, I was saddened by the prospect of having to abandon my tutors. John, my elder brother, thought me a fool. He was only too eager, two years earlier, to trade his books for a sword.

I remember so many evenings when our father, over a private family meal, would try to encourage my brother in his studies. "You may not think so now, Son," he'd say, "but when you take your place in the king's service, what you've learned will help you make wise decisions for our people."

"But isn't it just as important to do things that show the king's strength to the people and to our enemies?" John would counter. "*That's* the kind of service I want to do."

"Both are important," Father would always try to reason with him, "so you'd do well to prepare for whatever service your king might ask of you."

John's reply would always be something along the lines of "School is boring" or "The tutors don't give me good marks" or "I'd rather be outdoors" . . . any of which would typically lead my father in the same direction. "Perhaps the reason you don't get good marks, John, is that you don't really apply yourself. Look at Alfred. He studies and prepares his assignments and does very well. You could do the same if you just put your mind to it."

And just as predictably, at the end of the meal, when the two of us would return to the room we shared, the taunting would start. "Look at Alfred. He does very well," his tone mocking and jeering. "Why can't you just be like Alfred?" I knew better than to respond; I'd tried that once, several years ago, and wound up on the losing end of a fight.

It seemed Father finally got through to him shortly before his thirteenth birthday. It was our first private family supper after all the court celebrations of Christmas, New Year's, and Twelfth Night. Near the end of the meal, Father turned to me and asked something in Latin . . . I don't even remember what the question was . . . only that I replied in the same tongue and we continued in that vein for a bit. When my father paused for a sip of wine, John pounced. "Why don't you two speak so the rest of us can understand? Or is it because you're talking about me?"

"Perhaps if you'd studied your Latin, John, you'd be able to join the conversation rather than fret over it." I was puzzled by why my father seemed so unruffled; he usually got very frustrated and sometimes angry when John became insolent.

"I'm not going to be a churchman," my brother replied, "so why does it matter?"

"It matters, John," my father's tone remained calm but firm, "because you're a son of the royal house, and you're expected to have some Latin. Your tutor came to me today to complain that you're woefully behind in your progress, so I've decided you'll remain in school until he's satisfied with your mastery. If this means delaying your physical training until the following year, then so be it. The choice is yours. And I'll say nothing more on the subject."

John was so taken aback, he couldn't muster a response. But as soon as we were in the corridor on the way to our room, he rounded on me. "Show off!" he snarled. "Why do you always have to make me look bad?"

"All I did was answer Father's question. It had nothing to do with you."

"Maybe they'll give you to the Church after all, and then all that fancy Latin will actually do you some good." He stomped off down the corridor leaving me behind. I didn't bother trying to catch up; I knew from experience nothing good could possibly come of trying to talk to him when he was in one of his moods.

But my father's tactic worked. From that day until the end of the school term, my brother spent every waking moment studying his Latin and looked quite smug when the tutor pronounced that he'd mastered what a royal lad should know. He began his physical training that year and threw himself into learning the knightly skills with a gusto none of us had ever seen from him. Perhaps, I remember thinking at the time, he'd be happier now, and we could be better friends. For the next two years, that would prove to be the case.

And then it was my turn to follow in my brother's footsteps. I was determined to show my father – and my grandfather the king – that I understood my duty. So I did my best, even if I didn't share John's overt exuberance for all things of a knightly persuasion. I was joined in this adventure by sons of the lords who were at court, lads of an age with me. There were also some trainees for the knighthood in our group.

Sir Cedric was our trainer—a distinct honor for us, as Cedric is, even to this day, a legend in the kingdom because of what happened on the day of my grandfather's coronation. It was Sir Cedric's arrow that had wounded my great-grandfather, a wound that later festered and led to his death. Everyone believed Sir Cedric would be executed for killing the king, but my grandfather declared him innocent of any wrongdoing and proclaimed the whole incident to be a very unfortunate accident. He did this in the market square immediately following his coronation so the crowds would hear his judgment and know what kind of king he intended to be. The people cheered because Sir Cedric was very popular. But not everyone was happy. There were some among the back row of knights who swore they heard Sir Ranulf muttering to anyone who might be listening, "Nobody kills a king and gets away with it. That arsehole will pay. So will the arsehole who pardoned him." Many saw Ranulf turn on his heel and stride purposefully away from the crowd and out of the square, going who knew where. I wasn't there, of course; but the stories are so familiar that it almost seems as if I had been.

Horsemanship training was what I relished most. My grandfather is an expert horseman and I wanted to be just like him. "Your grandfather has a way with the animals," said Sir Cedric, "that makes it seem like horse and rider can read each other's thoughts. You'll have to work hard, lad, if you want to ride like the king." But I love these magnificent beasts, so it never seemed like work.

I didn't excel at wrestling; my mates bested me most of the time. We all laughed and joked, no matter who won or lost, but for me, it was humiliating to lose. And yet Sir Cedric kept pushing me to try harder. I could run more steadily and farther than many and could scamper over a fence, a low wall, or a hedgerow with ease. But we all found it much harder when carrying a heavy shield. We'd climb scaffolds, with and without the shields. We practiced with flails and war hammers and battle axes. And at the end of each day, I'd be more tired than I could ever have believed possible. On those days when I fell into bed without even undressing, John teased me, "Harder than you thought, eh, Brother?" He seemed to enjoy feeling superior because he'd already been at this for two years, but I was usually too exhausted to care.

My friend Samuel was good at everything. He'd already decided he wanted to be a knight, since he's Lord Ernle's third son and would have to make his own way in the world. Sometimes, when we were paired for an exercise, I suspected he let me win because I'm the king's grandson. "Why would I do that?" he replied when I asked him about it, but I was never sure I believed him.

There were times when I thought Sir Cedric expected more of me than of the other lads. I complained to my father about this but didn't find him particularly sympathetic. "You're a son of the royal house," he said. "Sir Cedric can't be seen to show you favoritism. For a knight, that would be dishonorable. And what would your friends think?"

"But he's harder on me than the rest," I protested.

"If that's true, then perhaps it's because he believes you more capable than the rest."

I remember crossing my arms in a huff, a gesture of which I knew my father disapproved, but I couldn't help myself.

"Have you considered talking with him about it?" he asked. "He may be your tutor now, but that won't always be so. He's one of the most respected men in the kingdom, and you could do worse than to have him as a friend."

I had never considered this possibility—either of talking with Sir Cedric or of ever being his friend. I couldn't imagine then that adults might ever see me as an equal. "Perhaps," I said.

But I decided instead to seek the advice of my grandfather. To this end, I spent more and more time in the library, often at the expense of sleep, in the hope of encountering him there. It was no hardship, really, for the library and all its books reminded me of the pleasant days of school. When at last my diligence was rewarded, I suddenly found myself timid about broaching the subject with him. I was reading a book in a chair before the hearth when he entered, selected his own book, and took a chair opposite me. As we sat in silence, each apparently absorbed in our own reading, I tried out in my mind what I might say to him. Everything I thought of seemed lame now that he was there.

Pausing in his reading, Grandfather looked up at me. "I've noticed you're spending quite a lot of time here lately, Alfred. What captures so much interest that you don't even escape to rest?"

"It's all interesting, sir. And there are so many books to read." My reply sounded childish, even to my own ears.

"I'm told by Sir Cedric that you're doing quite well in your training. That's high praise from such a distinguished knight."

My surprise at hearing him say this caused me to blurt out my first thought. "But sir, he's harder on me than the rest. I can't do anything to his satisfaction, and I can't do any more than I can do."

"In that, you're wrong, young Alfred. Has he not advanced you to the next level of horsemanship training?"

"Yes, sir," I replied.

"I'm not aware of any young trainee who's been advanced so quickly."

Suddenly I was beginning to feel rather sheepish about

complaining to my grandfather, but he didn't drop the subject. "You might not believe this, Alfred, but I completely understand what you're experiencing. When I undertook this training, I wasn't enthusiastic about it; but I understood it was necessary for my future role as king. It gets better when you take up archery and swordsmanship. You're already a skilled horseman, and there's no reason to believe you won't find other things you do very well indeed."

"But, sir, that's the future, and I don't know how to please Sir Cedric now." I tried not to whine.

"I believe your father suggested you talk with him. Have you considered that?"

"I don't know how to talk to him, sir. And I think my mates would think I'm taking advantage of being your grandson and then wouldn't be my mates any longer but would mock me."

"And how did you arrange to talk with me, Alfred?"

It surprised me to realize he knew I'd planned this encounter.

"I . . . I spent a lot of time in a place I knew you'd eventually come to. And I waited until that happened."

"Could you do the same with Sir Cedric?"

"I don't know where he likes to go."

"I understand you're to go on your first encampment soon."

"Yes, sir, that's right."

"I've asked Cedric to accompany me the next time I ride with a patrol to one of our market towns, about two weeks after your encampment. Do well in your exercise, and I'll invite you to join me. This would give you a chance to speak with Sir Cedric in private. Would that be satisfactory?"

I never dreamt this could be possible! To go on a patrol with my grandfather the king! I could barely contain my excitement. "I'll be perfect, sir, I promise. I'll do whatever Sir Cedric wants. I promise."

My grandfather smiled. "I'm sure you will, Alfred. And I look forward to going on patrol with you, too. Now off to bed with you and get some rest."

Thus began a pattern that my grandfather would repeat many times as I grew to manhood. He'd find me in the library and we'd talk of intellectual pursuits. He'd invite me on patrol and teach me to see the kingdom through his eyes. And he would always be present on the special occasions in my life. It would be many years before I understood why, but I relished every minute spent in his presence.

A week later, Sir Cedric gave us each a pack, with instructions that it must carry everything we thought necessary for an overnight patrol. "Report to me at the stable tomorrow morning at dawn," he said as he dismissed us for the day.

I spent the next several hours thinking of all the things I might possibly need and collecting them in my room. Blanket and pillow. A clean shirt and an extra pair of stockings. Two days' ration of oats for my horse. Dried venison, a small loaf of bread, a big chunk of cheese, and a sweet cake. Two water flasks. Four spare horseshoes, extra nails, and a small blacksmith's hammer. Four apples for me and my horse. Tinderbox. Leather gloves. Hobbles so my horse could graze unattended. My oiled-wool rain cape. A sharp knife. Two bottles of small ale. Brush and hoof pick to groom my horse. A spare bridle. Fishing line and hooks. A snare for catching rabbits. A cap for my head in case it rained. Tin drinking cup.

Sitting on the side of my bed, I was staring at it all . . . wondering what I might have forgotten and at the same time knowing even that lot wouldn't fit in the pack . . . when the door suddenly burst open and John marched in. "What in the name of all that's holy?" he exclaimed and then quickly realized what. "Oh, right. Your first encampment tomorrow. Do you really think you're going to take all that stuff?" And then he marched across the room, flung open the lid of his chest, and started rummaging about inside.

"Maybe you could tell me what's best to take. After all, you've done this lots of times."

No answer. Just more rummaging accompanied by indecipherable mumbling. And then "Aha, there you are!" He shook a pair of gloves in front of his face as if chastising them for having gone missing. Releasing the chest lid to shut with a resounding crash, he glanced in my direction. "*You*'re so smart. *You* figure it out. Just have this mess cleaned up before I come back." Then he stormed out of the room and slammed the door behind him.

What, I wondered, had happened to the brother who was my friend? A riddle I couldn't solve just then, so I turned my attention back to the task at hand and started trying to apply some logic to the problem.

I must eat, so the bread and dried venison were required; I wouldn't suffer without the sweet cake and cheese. I must drink, so a flask for water was required; but as we would be passing streams where I could refill it, I needed only one. On and on, choosing and discarding, until the pack was nearly full. In the last bit of space, I tucked two apples—rewards for me and my horse at the end of a long day's ride.

That night, my parents chose to join us for a private family supper rather than attend the court dinner. Father reminisced a bit about his first encampment and asked about my preparations. Mother tried to impress on me the importance of being careful and doing nothing dangerous or foolish. John sulked and said nothing.

When the meal was finished and John and I excused ourselves to leave, Mother said, "A word, please, Alfred?"

John glared at me, grunted "Hmph," and stomped away.

"Do you know what's bothering your brother?" Mother asked as soon as the door closed. "He's been so much more pleasant of late, and now this."

"I've no idea. He's been stomping around and slamming things all afternoon."

"Perhaps he'll tell you," Mother said. "All he'd tell me was that it wasn't women's business."

"I can ask."

"I intend to speak to his trainers in the morning," said my father, "but if you learn anything, let me know. I'll be at the stable before you leave. I want to nip this in the bud before it gets out of hand again."

When I got back to our room, John was pacing around, still fuming over whatever had set him off. Starting to undress, I asked, "Why are you so grumpy today?"

"What business is it of yours? Is that why they wanted to talk to you? 'Dear Alfred, do find out what's wrong with John,'" he mimicked our mother.

"No, it was something else entirely. I just like it better when we're friends." This was the first time I'd lied to my brother. If it got the information Father wanted, then perhaps it wasn't such a big lie? I knew what the priests would say. They'd say a lie is a lie . . . they don't come in sizes. But if I told the truth, John would shut me out completely, and then I'd have failed Father. Besides, the second half of what I said was true . . . I *did* like it better when we were friends. Was this, I wondered, what adults have to do to get information from each other?

Pulling my nightshirt over my head and climbing into bed, I tried again. "Come on, John. What are you fuming about?"

"Very well, if you must know, it's Guyat Bauldry." Lord Bauldry's heir.

"I thought he was your mate."

"He was. Until he had the unmitigated gall to beat me twice in a row in duels today. Doesn't he know he's supposed to defer to an heir to the throne?"

My impulse was to retort, "Since when are you heir to the throne?" But John *is* third in line of succession – for the moment at least – so I bit my tongue and replied simply, "Maybe it was just his day to be better at swordplay." Apparently not a much more palatable response, since he threw his pillow at me, flung himself into his bed fully clothed, and turned his back in my direction. Was it too much to hope that Father would get this sorted out before I returned?

It was a long day's ride—the longest any of us had ever spent in the saddle—but just an ordinary day, said Sir Cedric, for a knight on patrol. When the sun began to lower in the western sky, he called a halt in a meadow near a small grove of trees beside a stream. "Form your ranks," he ordered. We obediently formed two lines facing him but remained mounted.

"This will be our camp for tonight," he announced. "Would anyone like to say why your captain has chosen this spot?"

From Phillip, who sometimes fancies himself the court jester, "'Cause our arses are so sore from riding all day that we can't go any farther?" Everyone roared with laughter. Even Sir Cedric cracked a smile.

"Right, lads. At the end of a day's march, the Roman legions would construct a complete fortification for the night." Everyone groaned. Was he really going to make us build a fort?

"It is your captain's judgment, however, that we're safe enough here that an ordinary camp will suffice." Our noisy cheering brought another smile to his face.

While we were unsaddling and tending to our mounts, a lone rider, clearly a knight, approached from the north and stopped to greet Sir Cedric. "All well here, good sir?"

"Indeed it is, good sir. We have a fine camp and all that we need for the night. Good journey to you."

"Good evening to you," said the rider and continued on his way.

We caught fish and cleaned and cooked them and had a most excellent supper. A few of the lads had brought bottles of small ale and shared them around, with Sir Cedric's wholehearted approval. I went back to where I'd made a bed of my saddle and pack and blanket and retrieved the two apples. Then I found my horse, and we both munched contentedly on our apples until Sir Cedric called us to organize for the watch.

In groups of two, we would have an hour on watch while the others slept. Sir Cedric gave the sentries an hourglass. Phillip and I had the first watch and were told to wake Richard and Samuel when the hourglass emptied. Sir Cedric assigned the last watch to himself.

Exhausted from a long day in the saddle, sleep came easily to all of us. None of us ever told Sir Cedric that we may have dozed briefly while on duty, but in hushed conversations among ourselves, we all admitted remembering a knightly hand nudging us to wakefulness at some point near the end of our watch. We came to the conclusion that Sir Cedric didn't really sleep at all that night.

I learned later that the truth was somewhat different. Thirty minutes before our departure, a single knight had left the castle to scout the route we would travel, making sure no real danger lay in our path. An hour after we left, three more knights leading a pack horse loaded with provisions and supplies followed behind us and stopped out of sight, just inside the edge of the woods near our camp. The rider who greeted Sir Cedric was the first knight, who had doubled back to determine how well we were equipped for the night. If we had been woefully unprepared, Sir Cedric would have given him a different answer to his question, and he would've told his comrades in the woods to bring the pack horse forward. Had that been necessary, we would undoubtedly have spent a comfortable night, but would've received a remarkably uncomfortable tongue-lashing from Sir Cedric on our return home. As it was, the only job for the four knights was to stand watch over us throughout the night and gently wake us when we dozed while valiantly trying to be sentries. They woke Sir Cedric for the last watch and then returned to the castle with none of us the wiser for their presence.

True to his word, my grandfather the king invited me to join him on his next patrol. And much to my surprise, I learned my father was right about Sir Cedric believing me capable. I've since learned that Father was also right that the man who was my taskmaster then is now most assuredly my friend.

I did little else on this patrol other than to watch and observe. Grandfather invited me to dine with him and Abbot Francis whenever they weren't engaged with important people of the villages and towns we visited. Too soon, though, the two weeks were over, and ordinary life began anew.

For my fifteenth birthday, my grandfather gave me a weanling colt, a beautiful bay with a white crescent on his forehead, the son of his prize stallion out of his favorite mare. I named him Star Dancer, for he had the mark of the crescent moon and was given to me at a time when the crescent moon was traveling among the brightest stars in the sky.

"Raise him and train him well, Alfred," said my grandfather, "and he'll be a fine stallion for you for many years. Mervyn the Elder is still one of the finest horsemen I've ever known. If you agree, I'll ask him to guide you in training your horse."

I could think of nothing I'd like better but was so excited that the best I could manage was to nod my head vigorously.

"This means you'll have extra work every day."

"But it will be work I love, sir," I replied. "My colt is wonderful, and I'm going to make him the best horse in the stable."

Grandfather tousled my hair, smiled, and said, "Find Mervyn the Elder at the stable tomorrow. I've no doubt that the two of you will indeed make a fine mount of this youngster."

I quickly learned that training a horse is a great responsibility, starting with teaching him to like and trust me. "Best be if ye get him thinking ye come with his food," said Master Mervyn. So for the next week, I came to the stable early in the morning and again at sundown to feed Star Dancer. I'd sit on the ground at the entrance to his stall and hold his bucket of grain in my lap. At first, he was wary and wouldn't approach. "Ye be patient, lad," said Mervyn. "He be hungry, and soon he be figuring out he have to come t'ye if he be wanting to eat."

On the first morning, he was too shy. So Master Mervyn sent me on my way and later told me that Star Dancer ate his ration after I left. The same thing happened in the evening. On the second day, he stood off in the morning; but in the evening, he took a few tentative steps toward me, backed up, then came up and grabbed a mouthful of oats. After three more times like that, he decided no harm would come to him if he finished his supper in my presence. The next morning, he backed off only once before coming to me and finishing his entire ration.

His trust grew every day, and within a week, we'd gotten a halter on him, and he'd learned to walk with me on a lead. "He be a right smart one," said Master Mervyn. It would be many months before he was old enough to train to the saddle; but I spent time with him every day, and he came along whenever I went riding. "So's he be seeing the big world and learn it not be so fearsome," said Mervyn. Alas, this meant I always rode a mare, since he followed better if he thought my mount might be his mother.

Samuel and Richard were, even then, my best mates, and we did everything together. Richard would inherit the Devereux title one day. Sometimes Phillip, Lord Thorssen's heir, would join us. The Thorssen domain is in the southeast, on the sea coast, and from the castle tower there's a view for miles and miles out to sea in three directions.

We all had dogs. My father said we could go anywhere we wanted during the daytime . . . in the town and around the castle grounds and the nearby fields and woods . . . so long as the dogs were with us. Whenever we had any daylight hours free, we'd fetch the dogs and go off on our own. We liked to fish and sometimes we brought back a nice catch to give to the cooks. That usually earned us each a sweet cake as a reward.

We found a small stone hut in the woods not too far from the castle. Richard said his father thought it might have been a gamekeeper's hut once upon a time. We called it our lodge and kept our snares and traps there. Sometimes we'd catch a rabbit, but usually our traps were empty. Samuel thought that was probably because the dogs were there so much that the rabbits knew to stay away. That didn't stop us from trying, especially since a nice rabbit was good for both a sweet cake *and* a piece of fruit from the cook.

John was never very interested when I'd try to tell him about our lodge and how much we enjoyed it. "You'll grow out of that soon enough," he told me one night. "Then you can do things more fitting for a man." He'd decided that, at seventeen, he was already a man and boyhood pursuits were a thing of the past. Maybe he was right. After all, he would come of age in the following year.

He'd also decided he could do pretty much anything he wanted to with impunity. One night, he failed to appear at the court dinner. My grandfather noticed . . . how could he not, since we always sat directly opposite him in the dining hall. He didn't say anything, presumably not wanting to embarrass my father in front of the whole court. But he looked from John's empty seat to my parents and raised his eyebrows. Father shrugged; apparently, he didn't know where John was either.

Nor was he in our room when I went back there after dining. I spent half an hour reading a few pages of a book about Julius Caesar; but when he hadn't returned by then, I doused the candle, climbed into bed, and quickly fell asleep.

Sometime in the middle of the night, I woke to the door opening and closing loudly and the sound of John's boot steps on the floor. "Where've you been?" I hissed at him.

"What business is it of yours?"

"Grandfather noticed you weren't at the court dinner. You're going to be in trouble."

"Stuffy old court dinner." His dismissive tone was accompanied by the sound of one boot falling to the floor. "I'd rather be making the ladies happy." He paused. "Which – to answer your question – is where I've been."

"You mean . . . ?"

"That's precisely what I mean. Not that *you*'d be up to that sort of thing."

"What makes you think I can't?"

"Ooooooh. Feeling your oats already, Little Brother? Well, then, maybe sometime I'll just have to take you along and let you prove it. Not that the ladies would be interested in a skinny lad like you when they can have a real man." Another pause, punctuated by the second boot falling. "But then again, they can hardly refuse a grandson of the king."

The next evening, at our private supper in my parents' apartment, John was once again missing. Father sent his squire in search of him while we passed the time talking about my colt and what we were learning about swordplay. At one point, Father suggested we proceed with the meal, but Mother wanted to wait. "Let me deal with this as a breach of manners, Edward," she said. "You can chastise him later if he's been up to something he shouldn't."

After what seemed like an endless wait, there was a quick knock on the door before it opened and my brother entered, followed by my father's squire. John was clearly annoyed as he crossed the room and flopped down in the chair that was waiting for him. "I be finding him in the tavern, m'lord. And 'twere no way easy to drag him out of there. Ye be needing anything else, m'lord?"

"Not at the moment, Donal." The squire bowed and started to leave. "And Donal?"

"Aye, m'lord?"

"Thank you."

"And now," said Mother, "we can eat at last." She lifted her soup cup and sipped from it, the signal that the rest of us could begin our meal.

John brought his cup to his mouth, took a big swallow, and then grimaced as he placed the cup back on the table. "It's *cold*!" He practically spat the word.

"Well," said Mother, "you did keep us waiting for almost an hour. You really shouldn't be surprised."

"Send back to the kitchen for something hot. We shouldn't have to eat this swill."

"I'll do no such thing, John. The food was perfectly delightful when it first arrived, and I'll not insult the cook by sending it back when you couldn't bother to either be on time or have the courtesy to send your excuses in advance. If you want to eat, this is what you'll eat."

Father and I had no choice but to set a good example by tucking into our cold meal. John poked at the food on his plate with a knife then grabbed a piece of bread as if it were the only thing edible in the room.

"And while I'm on the subject," Mother continued, "have you forgotten all your court manners?"

"I'm sure I don't know what you mean, Mother."

"Failing to show up at the court dinner last night without sending your regrets to your grandfather in advance was boorish and quite unseemly for a son of the royal house. He noticed your absence, of course. You'll not embarrass your father and me like that again, do you understand?"

Busily chewing on a mouthful of bread, John managed only a mumbled, "Hm."

"Do you understand, John? I'll not have a repetition of last night's behavior."

"Oh, very well, Mother. I shall be a paragon of royal decorum." His voice fairly dripped with sarcasm.

"And you'll not use that tone with your mother," added my father. John had the good sense not to reply.

Mother must have thought she'd made her point because she changed the subject cheerily. "So . . . Donal said you were in the tavern. Do tell us what's new in the town."

"Well, there's a new barmaid. You should see her." He winked at me. "Just looking at her's enough to make a man's blood run hot."

I glanced at my father and could tell by the set of his jaw and the grim look on his face that he was seething over his son's deplorable choice of conversation in our mother's presence. Sensing this, Mother reached over and touched his arm gently, trying to calm him. "No doubt any young woman would be attracted to someone as handsome as you, Son," she said.

John sat up just a bit straighter in his chair, raised his chin, and cocked his head in reaction to what I'm sure he took as a well-deserved compliment.

"Just remember to be careful, though," Mother continued sweetly. "You wouldn't want the responsibility of a royal bastard, I shouldn't think." I recall watching John's face and seeing him struggle to figure out how to reply. "You *have* spoken to your father about such things, I trust?" Mother added.

Father relaxed completely, and there was a hint of amusement in his eyes. John was at a complete loss. The best he could come up with was, "Mother . . . Father . . . may I be excused?"

"Of course, dear," Mother replied. "You, too, Alfred, if you've finished your meal."

Knowing what a foul mood my brother was going to be in, I lingered just long enough to hear his boot steps stomp down the corridor before rising to follow. When I turned at the door to bid them good night, Father was giving Mother a very sweet kiss. Breaking his embrace, he said, "This won't be the last of it, Alice."

"Probably not," she replied, with a hint of resignation in her voice. "But at least he's on notice for a while." And then she added, "Goodnight, Alfred." My cue to leave and close the door behind me.

The following spring, I was ordered by my grandfather to accompany a trading expedition to the Kingdom of Peaks. My mates were to go as well. No doubt Grandfather thought he was giving us a reward for doing so well in our training, but I chose to think of it as a royal assignment. We'd be taking a stallion from my grandfather's stables to exchange for longbows. We'd also be taking a mare as a gift of friendship from our Council — the advisors to the king.

Originally composed of only the hereditary lords, the Council's makeup had changed over the centuries. Long ago, one of my ancestors convinced the lords that the lands and people of our original domain needed a voice, so a member of the royal family was added. My great-grandfather added the knight commander to advise on military matters and introduced the practice of lords rotating on and off the Council so that the group didn't become too unwieldy. As first lord of the realm, Lord Devereux is leader of the Council and has a permanent seat. Curiously, the royal family's seat is also permanent, and it seems there's never been any objection. My grandfather added the bishop. "The Church can be formidable as an ally or a foe," he once told me, "and they're more likely to be an ally if they believe decisions have been made with spiritual guidance."

We were told of the journey a week in advance, so I spent that week making friends with the stallion. I was at his stall every morning at feeding time; and after each day's training, I returned to give him an apple or a carrot and brush his coat.

On the day we departed, we assembled at the stable at dawn. My mates would ride big geldings, almost as large as the knights' stallions. Once again I was assigned a mare. Why was I always assigned a mare? Would this humiliation never end? As the captain gave the order to ride out, I remember thinking to myself about how I'd soon get some of my own back. How Star Dancer would soon be old enough and big enough to carry a man so I could train him to perfection and be the first of my mates to ride a magnificent stallion.

I suppose I had a scowl on my face, mulling over my humiliation and eventual revenge, for the knight riding next to me said, "Cheer up. You must think it quite an honor to be asked to ride the Council's gift horse."

Jolted from my thoughts by his words, I turned to him with a questioning look on my face. "Sir?"

"She's quite beautiful. It looks to me as if her gaits are smooth, so she must be a pleasure to ride." He paused to let me think about this. "And someone must think you're quite a fine horseman to trust you with getting her there without mishap."

His comments made me stop thinking about myself and take stock of my mount. A dapple grey with a long, lush, dark grey mane and tail that hearkened back to her ancestors from the southwestern part of my grandmother's homeland. And she did have the smoothest gaits I'd ever ridden. The notion that I was *allowed* to ride her rather than *required* to ride her is something that hadn't occurred to me. I sat up just a bit taller in the saddle, determined to ride her with pride and see her safely to her new home.

Just after midday on the second day of our journey, we were surprised by a flock of pheasants suddenly springing into the air less than two feet from the road. The knight holding the stallion was nearest the birds; and the sudden motion, the noise of flapping wings, and the birds in the air gave the stallion quite a fright. He reared, jerking the lead rope from the knight's hand, and galloped away across the field. Almost everyone immediately took off in pursuit. Only the knight with the pack horses and I remained quietly on the road.

The pursuers tried to circle around the stallion to herd him back toward us. They had him pointed in that direction, but as he approached the road, he recognized the place where the birds flew up, wheeled around, and ran the opposite way, right between his nearest pursuers. This wild frenzy of chase, encircle, and escape continued for several more attempts.

Finally, as the chase group came together again near the road, I screamed, "Halt!" at the top of my lungs. To my amazement, everyone's training kicked in, and they immediately froze in their tracks. Even the stallion slowed his pace to look at me. Immediately, I screamed, "Captain!" and, thankfully, the captain trotted over to find out why I'd chosen to disrupt his recapture efforts. As he neared, I held up my hand in an attempt to stave off a tongue-lashing and without waiting to be spoken to said, "This isn't working, sir."

"I can *see* that." His irritation was clear in his tone. "And I can also see you've interrupted us in trying to prevent him from being lost entirely. Perhaps you have some explanation?"

"Look, sir," I pointed toward the stallion, who'd stopped his frenzied running about and was walking quietly in the field watching us. "He's calming down already."

"Yes, I see. Now, may I assume you didn't stop our efforts to capture him without some sort of plan in mind?"

"We'll never catch him here, sir. He still remembers the birds flying up and frightening him in this spot."

"The lad makes sense, Captain," said the knight in charge of the pack horses.

"Aye, he does," agreed the captain, turning his attention back to me. "What do you suggest?"

"Leave me here with two feed bags and some oats. The rest of you ride on until you're completely out of sight . . . at least over that next rise up ahead. I've been feeding him and building his trust all this past week. Once the commotion has died down and he thinks we're alone, he'll come to me for food. I have some apples in my pack to tempt him with as well."

The captain looked doubtful and said nothing for quite some time.

"Besides," I added, smiling a little, "I think he likes this mare." We'd been riding just in front of the stallion, and I'd noticed him move forward and sniff at her haunches several times during the morning.

"The lad makes another good point, Captain," chimed in the knight. "I've been watching from the rear."

"So what you're suggesting," the captain finally said, "is that I abandon my responsibility for the most valuable part of this trade mission and proceed on the journey without the stallion, without the Council's gift, and without the king's grandson?"

"Put that way, sir, it does sound like an unwise choice. But I'll take responsibility for the king's valuable stallion, and no one else will have to answer to my grandfather."

"Put that way, sir," said the captain, "it seems you leave me very little room for argument." He paused briefly then added, "Especially as I have no better plan.

"Very well, let's get the lad two feed bags and some oats and be on our way. We'll wait for you until sundown and then return. If your plan hasn't worked by then, we'll simply have to devise a new plan."

"With respect, sir, if I haven't joined you by sundown, make camp and wait for us. He may not choose to come for his food until the light is right for his normal evening feeding. Tonight's a full moon and there are no woods for many miles on this road. It should be bright enough for us to ride to you even if we leave here near twilight. If we haven't joined you by sunrise, then I think it would be a good idea for you to return."

"As you wish. Best of luck to you, lad. Mervyn says you have a way with horses. Let's hope you have a way with this one." And with that he formed up the troop, and they started down the road away from us.

When they were out of sight, I rode over to a small group of trees about fifty yards from where the stallion was grazing, hobbled the mare, and set her loose to forage. It took all afternoon, the stallion moving ever so slowly toward the mare as they grazed. From time to time, she would nicker, calling him closer.

Watching them, I began to ponder what might happen if I didn't manage to catch the stallion. I'd be in trouble with these knights immediately, not to mention what would await me when we got back home. Despite my bravado to the captain, did I really think my grandfather would absolve him from responsibility – a grown man, a knight, a troop captain even – on the word of a sixteen-year-old? Even if that sixteen-year-old *was* the king's grandson? Truth be told, it didn't seem likely. So why, I wondered, did the captain go along with my scheme? Fortunately, my patience was rewarded and any dire consequences avoided.

The captain must have given orders for our arrival, because when we rode in an hour after sundown, everyone stopped in their tracks and the usual evening sounds of a camp went silent. I handed over the lead rope to the knight in charge of the stallion, and the horse went with him calmly, as he had on the previous evening.

Just after midday on the fifth day of our journey we crossed into the Kingdom of Peaks. By mid-afternoon, the road brought us to a wide valley with a lively stream on one side and hills rising to either side and ahead of us. To my surprise, the captain ordered a halt and the knights dismounted and begin to prepare a camp. My mates and I followed suit.

As I was brushing down my mare, I asked the man next to me, "Why are we stopping so early?"

"You'll see," he replied and continued grooming his own mount. "Normally, we'd have arrived here at sundown yesterday, but that bit of bother with the stallion put us a half day off schedule. You won't catch me complaining, though, about a few free hours not spent in the saddle." He grinned widely at the four of us, who were still thoroughly confused.

It being a warm afternoon, my mates and I decided to go for a swim in the creek. The water was surprisingly cold, and we learned it was fed by snow melt from the high peaks. Some of the men fished, in hope that it wouldn't be another night of dried venison. We found some summer berries and picked all the ripe ones. Someone else found some wild onions, so there'd be something to cook with the fish.

We finished our supper just as the sun was setting over the western hills. Perhaps it was because it had been such a lazy afternoon, but everyone seemed to want to stay around the camp fire rather than bedding down for the night. It was quiet, the only sounds being the crackling of the fire and the occasional nicker of a horse.

Then someone said, "There's the first one."

The man sitting nearest nudged me and pointed to the top of a hill that must have been a quarter mile or more distant. There, a huge fire had been lit. Soon, another fire appeared on a different hill farther from us, and that was repeated until there were bonfires on every peak as far as we could see. As we watched, the first fire eventually died out and the others followed suit in due course. No one spoke. My mates and I were dumbstruck by the spectacle we'd just witnessed.

When we could no longer see any fires, the knight said, "Impressive, eh?"

"What is it?" asked Richard.

"Signal fires, lad. They'll be lit on every hill top from here to the king's castle to announce our arrival. By the time we're ready to ride out tomorrow, the welcoming party will be here and we'll be escorted the rest of the way."

"Why is that?" asked Samuel.

"Used to be," said the knight, "there wasn't so much peace between our two kingdoms. These expeditions needed safe passage to protect us from attack from the hills on both sides of the road. Back in those days, a group like ours would wait here for an escort and then ride the rest of the way under the banner of the Peaks king.

"Nowadays, it's just ceremony. I've been with the captain on this trip five times now and I still love watching the fires light up. I'll tell you, though, if I were here on nefarious business, it would really make my skin crawl to see all those signal fires and know that everyone for miles around knew I was here."

Our escorts arrived, as predicted, just as we finished our preparations for departure. The two captains greeted each other as old friends. Protocol required that each member of our party ride beside a member of theirs, but it was more a demonstration of friendship than a necessity of survival.

It was a long ride to their castle, and we arrived just before sundown, which happens earlier among the hills, where the horizon is not so low and wide. After six days on the road, our horses were bedded down in comfortable stalls, and we were assigned sleeping quarters in the barracks. Supper was a generous spread in the knights' dining hall, with fresh meat, vegetables, freshly-baked bread, and ale. Small ale for my mates and me. A full stomach and a soft mattress meant I was asleep almost before my head touched the pillow.

I awoke at dawn to the captain shaking my shoulder. "I thought you'd want time to make sure the mare and stallion look their best to be presented to the king this morning."

Though I would have much preferred to stay in a warm bed, I knew he was right. Dressing quickly, I grabbed my brush and headed for the stable. A half hour later, back in the dining hall, I joined my mates for a breakfast of warm porridge and berries. We were just finishing when the captain approached. "Ready to go?" he asked.

"I'm not sure what you mean, sir."

"I mean are you ready to go with me to present the horses to the Peaks king?"

"If that's what you wish, sir."

"Come along, then, we can't keep them waiting. Richard . . . Samuel . . . Phillip . . . you too." We followed him back to the stable, where Elvin was waiting for us. The younger son of Mervyn the Elder, Elvin went to the Peaks with the first horses we traded to help them start their breeding program and never returned. He fell in love with the blacksmith's daughter, they married, and he was made permanent stable master to the king. Our languages are very different. Having made this trip several times, the captain spoke some of theirs, and we were told their king had a little of ours. Elvin, it seemed, helped out when there was an impasse.

We crossed the outer bailey and entered the main courtyard. After all the obeisances were complete, the king appraised the horses. "A fine animal indeed . . . a worthy addition to our stable," he declared of the stallion, then turned his attention to the mare. "And what of this horse led by young Alfred?"

The captain gestured to me and said, "Alfred?"

This was totally unexpected. I had no idea I'd be called on to speak and no instruction as to what to say. But I knew I couldn't remain silent. "A gift from our Council, Sire. She is four years old, and her ancestors came from the southwestern part of the Kingdom Across the Southern Sea. She is well trained to ride, but also of an age for breeding."

"I do not know when I have seen a prettier mare. If her gaits are as pleasing as her look, then perhaps I shall ride her myself." I was stunned. A king riding a mare? Did my astonishment show on my face? "For pleasure, of course," he added with a smile.

"I rode her on the journey, Sire. My disappointment in not getting to ride her back will only be bearable because I know she has a good home here."

Giving the horses into Elvin's charge, the king turned back to the captain. "Your longbows have been prepared for transport and are waiting for you at the stable. And we, too, have something special." He motioned to two squires, who came forward leading three dogs. "Our special breed of herding dogs. Legend says they were a gift to us from the fairy people who rode them as we ride horses. Look there," he pointed to one of the dogs. "You can see even now the mark of the fairy saddles." Indeed, the faint but distinct coat marking on the backs of all three did look remarkably like a miniature saddle.

"We offer these three as a gift and invite your king to consider a new arrangement whereby we would trade dogs for grain." From a pocket in his robe he retrieved a folded and sealed parchment. "A letter for your king containing my proposal."

As we prepared for departure, Elvin joined us. "A word with ye, Captain?"

"Of course, Elvin."

"Ye might be wanting to hear this, too, lad," said Elvin, beckoning us to a corner of the stable away from all the activity.

"I be thinking it best ye know. Ranulf and his sons be seen in the high peaks near our border with the Kingdom of Lakes."

"Are you certain?" asked the captain. "The last we knew, they were in the wilds at the northern border of the Lakes."

"Seems they've come south," replied Elvin.

"How sure are you that it's really them?"

"I canna' be fer certain sure. But it be an older man and three younger ones. They say the older man have a scar on his cheek just like what Ranulf got in the duel over that girl. They say, too, the four be talking like ye'd talk with me and not like the Peaks folk."

"Could be a dialect from the Lakes. Our languages are pretty similar."

"Like I say, sir. I not be seeing or hearing them meself so I canna' say fer sure. But I be thinking ye want to know."

"That's true enough, Elvin. We'll see what we can find out. And if you learn anything more, find a way to get word to us. We'll do the same."

"Aye, I be doing that. That bunch be trouble no matter where they be."

I'd been wondering how we would travel with the dogs, but that was solved in a most ingenious manner. A small cart fitted with an open cage on the top allowed them to see out but not jump out. The cart had a long piece of wood cleverly mounted underneath and extending well out to the left, and with a long handle attached. A lead rope tied to the handle let a rider pull the cart without its interfering with the horse's movement.

The captain put the four of us in charge of the dogs for the return journey, and we spent the time choosing the best and noblest names for them. One of the bitches had many white markings in her coat, so we settled on Luna for her, in honor of the moon goddess. The other bitch we named Morgana, to honor the Queen of the Kingdom of Peaks. Choosing a name for the dog proved more difficult. We tried many things that either didn't fit him or didn't satisfy us. Finally, on the last day of the journey, Richard was inspired. "Let's name him in honor of Sir Cedric," he suggested, to which we all agreed. And so, six days after we started out, as the sun was lowering in the western sky, we rode into my grandfather's stable with fifty longbows, eight sacks of the finest arrows, and with Luna, Morgana, and Cedric barking excitedly in their cart.

Two days afterward, I received an invitation to dine with my grandfather and the captain of the expedition. My father couldn't decide if I was in trouble or if this was some sort of honor and fretted throughout the day over what might be about to happen to me.

Dressed in my finest clothes, I arrived at my grandfather's chambers precisely on time, only to find that the captain was already there. Apparently, this was by pre-arrangement, for my grandfather praised me for being punctual.

As the first course was being served, Grandfather poured wine into my goblet. A first . . . I was usually given small ale. "Perhaps you should water it a bit since this is your first time," he suggested. I nodded, and he poured a bit of water into the wine.

Grandfather raised his glass. "To a most successful expedition." The captain raised his glass and touched it to that of my grandfather. I followed suit and imitated them as we drank the toast. The taste of the wine was both odd and delightful, but I imagined I'd grow to like it with experience.

As we wiped our soup bowls clean with a crust of bread, the servants brought a roasted pheasant and carved it before us, placing a generous serving on each plate. "I thought pheasant might be a fitting choice," said Grandfather, "since it played such a role in the adventures of your journey."

"His Grace invited me to give him an accounting of our expedition," said the captain.

"I'm told you acquitted yourself admirably," added my grandfather.

Finishing my morsel of pheasant, I replied, "Sir, I've been wanting to speak with you. I must admit I was insubordinate when the stallion escaped. The captain was very tolerant of my behavior, and we were fortunate that all ended well." I tried to put the best face possible on things, so as not to be in any more trouble than absolutely necessary, and gave credit to the captain.

"As I understand it," said my grandfather, "you were quite brave. It takes courage, Alfred, to challenge authority. Why did you do it?"

"It was the right thing for the horse, sir. There wasn't going to be a good outcome if the chase continued."

"I see. And what would you have done had the captain not gone along with you?"

"I'm not sure, sir. I didn't have to think about that."

"Think about it now."

I chewed a morsel of pheasant and washed it down with a sip of wine while my mind was racing. "I think I should have done what I did after they left . . . ride to the trees and take out my apples and try to entice the stallion to come to me and the mare."

"And if the stallion didn't respond? If he was still too caught up in the frenzy of being chased?"

"Well, sir, if some of the others had seen the rightness of what I was doing, we might still have recaptured him. But at some point, I'd have had no choice but to obey my captain."

"How would you have felt about that?"

"I don't know, sir. If the stallion had been recaptured, I'd have been relieved; but I don't think I'd have liked the way it was done. If he'd escaped completely, I'd have been very sad indeed and would've had to apologize to you for not being able to take care of him properly."

"Why would you feel that responsibility, Alfred? You weren't in charge of the expedition."

"I'm your grandson, sir, and he was your horse."

We finished our meal in silence, and the servants refilled the glasses of my grandfather and the captain. Pushing his plate away to indicate he'd finished, Grandfather said, "Alfred, I'm quite proud of your behavior on this expedition. Your instincts served you well. The captain tells me you intended to absolve him of any blame if your plan had failed." He paused. "I'm not sure I would have been so generous." He paused again for a sip of wine.

"Yes, sir," I replied.

"I want to add," said the captain, "that I was much impressed with you, Lord Alfred." How clearly I remember my reaction! I was stunned. This was the first time anyone had used that title with my name, though it's my right as a son of the royal family. "I'd be honored to ride again with you whenever we have the opportunity."

"And I'd be honored to ride with you as well, sir."

"And now," said my grandfather, "tell me what you thought of my mare. I made special arrangements for you to ride her, you know."

Another surprise. How many more were there to be this evening?

"She was remarkable, sir. I've never ridden a horse with such smooth gaits. And she seemed to be able to read my thoughts. Without her, I don't know if I could have recaptured the stallion so easily."

"She was one of my favorites. It was really quite difficult to part with her."

"For me, too, sir; but I know she's in good hands with Master Elvin. And she'll breed some beautiful foals for the Peaks king."

We continued talking of horses over pudding and fruit. We talked of Star Dancer's training. My grandfather and the captain spoke of the coming tournament.

When Grandfather indicated the end of the evening, the captain and I departed together. As we went our separate ways, he said, "Good evening, Lord Alfred."

"Good evening, sir."

Walking back to my room, I thought about everything I'd learned over the past two weeks. Not to always take things at face value . . . sometimes there's an entirely different reason for what's happening than the first one that comes to mind. Sometimes other people are looking out for you without your even knowing it. I had thought to be chastised for my actions when the stallion escaped, even though the outcome was good. Yet my grandfather and the captain both praised me. And when I was placed in the totally unexpected situation of presenting the mare, I managed not to make a complete fool of myself. I rather suspected that was contrived as well, but it was gratifying to know I'd passed the test. And tonight, I was treated with respect by my grandfather and the captain – even called by my hereditary title for the first time – and had my first glass of real wine, watered though it may have been. I smiled to myself and thought that perhaps I really was coming of age.

The following year, Lord Montfort joined the Council. His eldest son Laurence joined him at court . . . and joined our little band of mates. Though Laurence was almost a year older than us, Sir Cedric agreed he could join our training as well.

That was also the year when Star Dancer was old enough to be ridden. When the day arrived that I was to ride him for the first time, all my mates were at the stable, waiting. I was certain they were there to laugh at me should I be thrown. So whatever apprehension I might have felt about this first ride turned into fierce determination not to give them cause for anything but admiration of my superior horsemanship. They greeted me with great slaps on the back and words of support, but I still suspected their motives.

With Master Mervyn's help, I'd taught Star Dancer to accept a saddle and even the weight of a rider, all within the confines of the stable, but today I was finally going to ride him in the arena. "It be different fer him out here, lad," said Mervyn. "He not be feeling so safe as in the barn. D'ye want to be the first to be riding him?"

"I think so," I replied.

"Then remember this. He be feeling safer if there be something solid on one side. Mount him here next to the fence. Then ride beside the fence half way down. If naught bad be happening, stop there and dismount and soothe him. Then lead him back here."

I could tell Star Dancer was more nervous outside the stable. He crowded the fence, and I had to struggle to keep my right leg from being bruised and battered. After a couple of short walks to and fro, he seemed to be gaining confidence, so I turned him away from the fence. He took a few steps then began a sort of dance. Fearing he might try to throw me, I reached forward and stroked his neck. He tried to rear; but since my weight was already forward, I didn't fall off. And when I moved my hand and sat straight in the saddle, he calmed. I dismounted and led him back to Master Mervyn.

"First time he be seeing a hand come from that direction, lad. But ye stayed on and kept him calm. He be remembering that."

On the third try, Star Dancer crossed the arena calmly at my direction. But as we were riding down the fence on the opposite side, he spied my four mates sitting there; and when one of them waved at us, he took off at a run. I hung on for dear life and, just as I thought I was about to be thrown, he slowed to a trot near the end of the arena. I collected my wits, slowed him to a walk, and returned to Master Mervyn, who was all smiles.

"Ye be making a fine pair, ye two. And I be thinking that be enough fer the first day."

I met my mates outside the stable. "You *idiots!*" I chided them. "Were you trying to scare him into throwing me off?"

They roared with laughter, and I could tell they'd have been delighted no end to have seen me on my arse in the dirt. Then it was all back slaps and congratulations as we went off in search of food and small ale to celebrate.

I still accompanied my grandfather occasionally on his travels within the kingdom. Once, I ventured to ask a question that had been puzzling me for some time. "I've been wondering, sir, why it is that you include me on these journeys but not John. After all, he's closer to the throne than I am."

We rode for quite some time in silence. I was beginning to fear I'd offended him in some way and was on the brink of opening my mouth to apologize when he said, "What do you think John would learn from these experiences?"

It was my turn to pause. I knew what I wanted to answer but was uncertain of my grandfather's opinion of my brother. Finally, I said, "I think not much."

"I'm afraid I share your opinion," said my grandfather, "which is why I no longer invite him on these journeys. I invited him three times, and he always found some reason to decline . . . all of which, I later discovered, were complete fabrications." What was John thinking that he would have the nerve to lie to Grandfather?

We rode on in silence for some time before he resumed. "I'm afraid John is self-centered and weak-minded. And that's a dangerous combination. Should he ever ascend the throne, the kingdom will need many wise men to protect it from whatever mayhem John might create, either intentionally or thoughtlessly. That's why I spend time with you and why I'm pleased with your choices of companions."

We said no more on the topic. I had learned that my grandfather liked to plant seeds of ideas and allow them to germinate as I pondered them over time. That's certainly something John would never have grasped.

The dogs we brought back from the Peaks were put in the care of the monastery, where Abbot Francis established a breeding kennel and placed Brother Adam in charge. I often wondered why my grandfather decided to proceed with the trade arrangement even before we knew if it would be successful. "I've been wondering, sir," I asked him one day, "how one knows when to take a risk when the outcome can't be easily foreseen."

"That's a question men have been wrestling with for centuries," he replied. "And one for which I make no claim to having a good answer. What prompted you to ask?"

"Well, this new trade agreement—grain for dogs," I said. "By the time we know whether or not we have a use for these dogs, it will have been almost two years since the original proposal. Yet you decided to proceed, have conducted the first trade, and are preparing for the second one. How does one come to such a decision in the absence of all the facts?"

"It's rare, Alfred, to have all the facts. But often there are more facts available than might appear at first glance. You're considering this, I think, through the lens of use and value. Why would we trade something of infinite use and value, such as food, for something that the use and value is still in question, such as the dogs? Am I correct?"

"That's right, sir."

"Let me suggest an additional perspective," he said. "I strongly applaud the Peaks king's desire to ensure his people have sufficient food. There are many things that motivate a man, but the most fundamental is survival. Only when survival is assured can a man consider such things as improving his status in life. And only when he's reasonably comfortable can he begin to consider greater contributions to society or helping to improve the lot of his fellow man.

"Since food is the most fundamental requirement for survival, there's nothing more dangerous than a starving man. He'll turn on his leaders, his friends, and his neighbors—whether they are next door, in the next town, or in the next kingdom—to get food.

"We're fortunate. We haven't had to confront hunger here for a very, very long time. So with survival assured, our people have turned their attention to improving their status. You see it in the increase in literacy and in the flourishing of commerce and trade in our towns."

"But, Grandfather, you and Abbot Francis provided the schools to improve literacy."

"And there you have part of the essence of what it is to govern. Illiterate people would have struggled to figure out how to achieve literacy on their own. By providing the means, we accelerated progress.

"But back to your dilemma of risk taking. The single most important fact I considered is what the Peaks king is trying to achieve by ensuring the food supply for his people. So, to the degree that we can support that goal without endangering our own kingdom, I'm happy to trade some of what we have in abundance for something that they value.

"No, we don't know yet whether we'll value these dogs in the same way. But if it transpires that we do not, agreements can always be modified. There's no doubt some other trade arrangement can be found that would suit us both."

I pondered this for a moment trying to work out my next question, but he continued. "Another thing to consider is whether or not one has a path forward no matter what the outcome of the decision. In this case, both Lord Thorssen and Francis have agreed to use the dogs with their flocks even if the other herdsmen won't accept them. So, when I agreed to the proposal, there was really very little risk at all.

"The fact that you ask, Alfred, tells me you're ready to take on a bigger role in making this arrangement successful. I'm putting you in charge of the kennel. Work with Brother Adam. Engage your mates to help you if you wish. Create a plan for the dogs for now and for the future and bring it to me a month hence." And that is how I came to be Patron of the Royal Kennel, my very first royal appointment.

Not long after that, my parents began preparing to celebrate my coming of age. There would be a feast for the entire court, a tournament, and a horse race. I convinced my father that the horse race should include hurdles and jumps, so that my mates and I could compete much as we practiced in the fields. My mother and the ladies of the court would require new gowns. A hunt was organized to ensure sufficient meat for the feast. There were tournament rules to be devised, contestants to be entered, pavilions to be erected, lodgings to be readied for all the visitors. A colossal undertaking, not unlike what I remembered two years previously for John's coming of age.

Unlike my brother's celebration, however, where I was a willing, if not enthusiastic, participant, John wanted nothing to do with mine and spent most of his time away from the castle, only occasionally coming home to sleep in his own bed. Then one evening he came to our room just as I'd returned from the evening meal. "Come on, Alfred, time to go for a proper celebration." I had rarely seen him so expansive.

"A what? Where?"

"The tavern. Come on. Let's go."

I recall having a decidedly uneasy feeling about his intentions.

"Come on, Brother. The longer we stay here, the more someone else is going to drink the ale *we* should be downing." Before I could say anything more, he was already halfway out the door, beckoning me to follow.

Unable to come up with a good reason why I shouldn't have a drink with him, I reluctantly put my boots back on and joined him. All the way there, he talked non-stop about how special his own coming-of-age celebration was, how he'd decided he wanted to find a wife or maybe be a knight or maybe just do nothing at all, but in any case, Father couldn't tell him what to do any longer because he was his own man now and I soon would be too. I recall wondering how many drinks he'd had at the tavern before deciding to come get me.

When we got there, the barmaids fawned all over him and brought us mugs of ale without our even ordering. "And this," he raised his mug to me, "is my little brother. Not so little any more, is he? Not quite as handsome as me, though, right, ladies?"

The dark-haired barmaid sat in his lap while the blonde one attempted to do the same with me. I tried to decline. "Come on, Brother. Don't insult a lady if she likes you." And now I knew exactly where this was going. Should I go along? Or make a scene with John here in public? If I went along, would everyone think I was just like my brother? But making a scene would be unbecoming for a royal. Either way, I risked embarrassing my family.

By now, the decision was out of my hands. The girl was in my lap, her ample bosom right in my face, one finger twirling my hair; and my body was responding in spite of myself. She jumped up, grabbed my hand, and tugged me off the stool and toward the stairs. "Have a good time," John laughed.

I followed her upstairs, thinking I could back out at the last minute if I wanted to. She led me into a room, closed the door behind us, and pushed me over to sit on the bed. "You don't have to do this," I told her.

Her reply was to open her bodice, freeing her breasts and bending over to bury my face in them. "What girl wouldn't want to bed the king's grandson?" she murmured. Then she dropped to the floor, tugged off my boots, and opened my trousers. Hiking up her skirt, she pushed me back on the bed and took matters into her own hands. I was completely out of control, giving myself up to the sheer pleasure of it all. And when it was over, I fell into an exhausted sleep.

Sometime later, I woke to find another of the barmaids in bed beside me, caressing my chest and kissing my forehead. My body had already reacted as if it couldn't possibly have been completely satiated just a short time ago. She rolled onto her back and I took her quickly, but this time, I willed myself not to fall asleep. Kissing her on the forehead, I sat up, pulled on my trousers and boots, and headed for the door. As I started down the stairs, I saw John stumbling down the last few steps and hurried to catch up with him. "Let's go home, Brother."

"Let's go home, Brother," he said just a little too loudly, weaving a bit as we made for the door. Walking across the square, he put his arm around my shoulder and said, "Well done, Brother." Then, raising his voice just a little too loudly for this hour of the night, "Hey, everybody, my brother!" Then he turned his attention back to me, "About time you had some fun, Alfred."

We made our way out of the town and onto the road up to the castle without drawing any further attention to ourselves, but as we walked along the road, John started singing. Some sort of bawdy drinking song I'd never heard before. He slapped me on the back so hard I almost fell over. "Come on, Brother. Sing!" Then he resumed his singing, oblivious to the fact that I hadn't joined him.

I managed to get him up the stairs and into our room where he fell onto his bed fully clothed and was snoring before I got across the room to my own bed. Taking off my boots, I wondered what I'd think about all this in the morning. I wondered, too, what John would think. Would he be my brother, my friend once again? Or would he revert to his sullen resentment of the fact that so much attention was being directed my way at the moment? John was right about one thing though: doing it with a woman is ever so much better than just taking care of things by yourself.

A week before my birthday, Grandfather invited my parents and me to dine with him. I had a feeling my parents knew what this was about, but they revealed nothing. After the last course, my grandfather invited us to gather around the fireplace and ordered a servant to bring wine. I ended up in a chair opposite him with my parents seated on a couch between us.

"It's not long now until your celebration, Alfred," said my grandfather. "There's something I'd like to do in private before the public presentation at the feast."

"Yes, sir," was all I could say, having no idea what was about to transpire.

"You know that part of the coming-of-age ceremony for a son of the royal house is the awarding of your symbol for your shield and coat of arms." I remembered this presentation to John. "I want you to know in advance what that will be so that you have time to prepare for whatever reaction may occur."

"Why should there be a reaction, sir? After all, I'm not particularly close to the throne. And my symbol is not of my own choosing, but awarded by my king."

"That remains to be seen, Alfred, because the symbol I've chosen for you is a rare one, not used in this kingdom since long before the days of my father's grandfather."

He paused, and I remained silent. Then he continued quite formally. "Lord Alfred, you are to be awarded as your symbol the lion dormant on a field of azure. You shall be the only member of this house save the king and the first two in line of succession to have a lion symbol. I've made the choice of a lion because of a sense that you are destined for some form of greatness. And I've chosen the lion dormant because that destiny is not yet apparent, but I believe you will be prepared to rise to it when it becomes clear."

My parents clearly had not been expecting this. Mother uttered a slight gasp of astonishment at the news. Father seemed to be trying to suppress a broad smile of pride. I was at a loss for words but somehow managed to utter the formal, "I'm honored, Your Grace."

"Now, Alfred," said my grandfather, "as we've dispensed with the formalities, we should discuss whether you feel prepared to handle this honor. You need not answer tonight. In fact, I'd very much like you to think carefully about the implications."

"I'm . . . I'm not sure what to ponder, sir," I replied, "since everyone should understand this is not of my choosing."

"True as that may be, Alfred, human nature often supersedes rational thought where such things are concerned. Some may be jealous — John comes to mind. Some may imagine I have hidden intentions of altering the succession, others that you somehow connived to achieve this. There'll be those who believe this means you have my ear and that they can use you to seek favors from me. Most, I hope, will simply celebrate your new status and treat you no differently than ever in the past.

"I'm convinced you have the maturity to cope with whatever reaction there is, else I wouldn't have made this choice for you. But I want the final decision to be yours. Give it some serious thought . . . talk it over with your father . . . and return to dine with me three days hence with your answer. There's no dishonor in asking me to select a different symbol for you. But it's my fervent hope that you find yourself able to accept the one I've chosen."

As I'm sure he intended, he succeeded in planting doubt in my mind. But was his point that I should turn that doubt into resolve? I limited my reply to a simple, "Yes, sir."

My grandfather smiled broadly and raised his glass. "To Alfred," and my parents joined him in the toast. "And now," he continued, "I believe your father has more for you to think about."

I would have a squire, chosen by my father and Sir Cedric. Cedric was teaching him martial skills and Donal was instructing him in the duties of a squire. Osbert would enter my service on the day of my birthday celebration.

I would also have my own apartment within the castle. "Apartment" is perhaps too grand a word for what is simply a larger bed chamber with dressing rooms. But it would be my private space, and my dressing room would provide sleeping quarters for my squire.

"And finally," my father began . . .

There seemed to be no end to the evening's surprises. And this was the greatest of them all. I was to be married!

I shall never forget the first time I laid eyes on the woman who would become my wife. It's etched in my memory as deeply and permanently as the stone carvings that grace the altar and chapels of the church. When the messenger arrived with the news that her traveling party would arrive mid-afternoon, Grandfather ordered Sir Cedric to assemble a guard of honor to join me to meet them outside the town. All my mates insisted on coming along.

I had no idea what to expect. Father had given me assurances this would be a good match. Lady Gwendolyn. Daughter of a noble house of the Kingdom of Lakes. Her father, Lord Godwin, a nephew of their king. An educated woman. A worthy addition to our family.

But he also said something extraordinary. "You should know, Alfred, that if this match is not to your liking, I'll not hold you to the contract. Godwin understands this, so you need only say if there's something you find unsuitable about the lady or the arrangement." If he meant this to be reassuring, it had quite the opposite effect. Would my betrothed be unattractive? Homely, even? Would she be unclean and smelly? Proud and haughty? Selfish and demanding? Crude and boorish? What might I discover that would lead me to ask my father to actually break his word in a marriage contract?

As we rode behind Sir Cedric, my mind was a jumble of excitement, anticipation, anxiety, and trepidation. About a quarter hour outside the town, we met the travelers, a man and his squire on horseback in the lead.

"Lord Godwin, I presume?" said Sir Cedric.

"Aye."

"Compliments of Lord Edward and my lord the king, I am Sir

Cedric, and we're here as your escort to the castle."

"We're most gratified, Sir Cedric." He motioned for his squire to move aside and an angel on horseback moved up to join him. "My daughter, Lady Gwendolyn. My lady wife and youngest daughters travel in our coach."

She was the most beautiful creature I had ever seen. To call her hair blonde would be to seriously understate the myriad colors that play among her tresses—brownish gold like the color of a well-used coin, the warm sunny shades of fresh honey, occasional strands that look like purest spun gold, and, here and there, just the very slightest hint of copper—all in a thick, lush mass of curls and softness. A golden contrast to the dark hair and blue eyes that predominate in my family. Eyes that are blue—bluer, even, than my own—and that sparkle like jewels. Taller than many women, which suits me well for I am taller than most men. In that moment I was completely enchanted. She sat her saddle with ease, like a natural horseman, her back straight but not rigid, her hands gentle on the reins. I could not take my eyes off her.

"Lady Gwendolyn," said Sir Cedric, "allow me to introduce your escorts." He introduced my mates then beckoned me to join him. "And finally, my lady, Lord Alfred, son of Prince Edward and Lady Alice, grandson of our king, Patron of the Royal Kennel, and your husband to be."

I dismounted, walked to her side, bowed deeply, and kissed her hand as warmly as I knew how. Behind me, Phillip's voice, "And somehow, amidst all that grandeur, it seems he's actually learned some manners," prompting laughter from all my mates.

"I'm delighted to meet you at last, Lady Gwendolyn. My parents tell me we met once as children, but I must admit I have no recollection."

"Nor do I," she replied, "though my parents have given me similar assurances. I, too, am pleased to meet you at last."

"Will you join me for the ride to the castle?" She guided her mare forward as I remounted my own horse. The guards in the rear moved aside as we reorganized the procession with Sir Cedric once again in the lead, Lady Gwendolyn and I immediately behind him.

"This lot . . . ," I turned in the saddle to gesture toward my mates, who'd fallen in right behind us. "This lot and I have somehow managed to become great friends, despite the fact that they once tried to get my horse to dump me on my backside in the dirt."

"You'd have been there, too, if the horse hadn't slowed down," said Samuel, prompting another round of laughter. Gwendolyn smiled. I was relieved that she didn't seem put off by the fun they were having at my expense.

"Nevertheless," I continued, "I hope that once you know them better, you'll like them as well as I do."

"No doubt I shall," she replied. Her voice was sweet and gentle – melodic, even, though some of that impression may have come from the naturally song-like accent of the Lakes people.

"I should tell you, there are crowds all along the streets through the town hoping to catch a glimpse of you. You honor me that you've chosen to ride openly rather than remain in the coach. We haven't had a royal betrothal or wedding since my uncle Rupert was married before I was even born, so everyone's in a festive mood."

We rode on in silence for a while until she chose a topic of conversation. "Your horse is most impressive. He seems quite content to ride alongside my mare, though he's never seen her before today."

"His name is Star Dancer. He was a gift from my grandfather. Your mare reminds me of one I once rode on an expedition. She seems to have the smooth gait and full mane of the horses from the Kingdom Across the Southern Sea."

"You're quite observant. Her name is Moon Gazer. She was born under the full moon, and when she was young, I often found her gazing up at the moon when I'd visit her in the evening."

"Do you think perhaps the similarity of their names bodes well for our future?"

She laughed softly. "I suppose the soothsayers might think so."

"And do you believe in soothsayers, Lady Gwendolyn?"

"Hardly." Her smile was beautiful. "How could anyone possibly foretell the future?" Then her expression darkened, as if she feared she might have said something wrong.

"In that case," I told her, "I think we've found the first thing that we have in common, my lady." And the smile returned.

As we approached the town, Sir Cedric turned in his saddle. "We've nearly arrived, my lady. If you're agreeable, we'll walk slowly through the market square. But if there's too much crowding or if you feel in any way uncomfortable, you need only signal Lord Alfred or me, and we'll increase the pace and move on to the castle."

"I'm sure it will all be quite pleasant, Sir Cedric, but thank you for your consideration."

The square was filled with cheering people. Many reached out to touch her skirt, but it was all with great respect, and there was no effort to crowd our horses or impede our progress. A few children reached up to offer her small bouquets and she collected as many as she could reach while staying securely in the saddle.

It was then that I noticed Cedric point toward some men at the edge of the crowd and order two of his men to go investigate. By the time the guards arrived, the men had fled. But Gwendolyn didn't fail to take note of what was happening. The crowds continued along the short road from the town to the castle, and I was grateful that they provided a distraction from the incident in the square.

The family had gathered in the inner courtyard to receive our visitors, and it naturally fell to me to introduce Gwendolyn to everyone in turn, ending with my grandfather. She curtsied deeply and held it until the king reached down to lift her up. "You're to be family, my dear. I believe we can dispense with the most formal of protocols."

It was then but a week until my birthday celebration, and the days were consumed with preparations. The final hunt, the last minute arrangements for the tournament, moving into my new apartment, becoming acquainted with Lord Godwin. Though I saw my betrothed at mealtimes, she was, during those days, mostly in the company of my mother and the ladies of the court.

The day of the event dawned cloudy, but by the time everyone was assembled in the pavilions at midday, the sun had triumphed and a light breeze gave a gentle flutter to the dozens of banners around the field. Though still called a tournament, this one included no jousting or mêlée—just competitions in military skills, demonstrations, and a horse race. Laurence bested John in a competition of swordplay, leaving him disgruntled and pouty. Following a demonstration by a group of longbowmen, the marksmanship competition ended in a tie between Samuel and me.

As we prepared for the horse race, most of the riders were already wearing tokens from their ladies, but I'd saved my grand gesture for the last minute. Gwendolyn was seated in the pavilion next to my grandfather, and I fancied she looked rather dismayed that I'd not yet asked to carry hers. Time to end the suspense. I rode up to the pavilion and stopped directly in front of her. "My Lady Gwendolyn, may I have the honor of carrying your favor in the race?" And then I coaxed Star Dancer down into an elaborate bow.

"My grandson seems to be quite the show-off where a beautiful lady is concerned," said Grandfather, as Gwendolyn stepped to the edge of the pavilion and tied a green silk scarf around my neck. I kissed her hand and trotted off to join the others at the starting line.

This was the first time we'd run a race like this, with hurdles set up at various points on the course. The rules were that if a horse refused a jump or knocked over a hurdle, the rider must pull up and drop out of the race. Three circuits to determine the winner. As we neared the finish, Phillip, Richard, and I were three abreast, urging our horses forward at top speed. At the last instant, Star Dancer won by a nose. No doubt they let me win. But since it was my birthday, I didn't chide them for their generosity.

The banquet was sumptuous indeed, the great hall packed with tables and benches on one side with space for entertainments and dancing on the other. The order of precedence was set aside in honor of the special nature of this celebration. Gwendolyn and I were seated on either side of my grandfather, with our parents next to us. There was soup and fish and pheasant and venison and roast boar. Beans and potatoes and carrots. Fruits of all sorts, including figs imported from the Kingdom Across the Southern Sea. Breads and cheeses.

Sweet cakes and puddings and tarts. Wine and cider and ale. Musicians played as we dined.

Finally, Grandfather rose, the music stopped, and the noise of conversation quickly subsided. "Tonight, we honor my grandson, Alfred, on the occasion of his eighteenth birthday. According to our traditions, this is the day we reveal his symbol by presenting him with a new shield."

Sir Cedric entered the great hall carrying a shield embossed with the image of a lion dormant on a field of azure, and I stepped down from the dais to stand beside him. A murmur of whispering ran through the hall as the assemblage saw the symbol for first time. The king raised his hand for silence. "Lord Alfred, accept this shield and swear your fealty to this realm."

I took the shield and dropped to one knee. "I swear my lifelong fealty to this kingdom, its people, and its king, Your Grace."

"Rise, Lord Alfred. I know not what your destiny shall be, but I am confident you will be ready when it presents itself." He then raised his glass, a signal that everyone else in the room should do the same. "Lord Alfred."

The crowd echoed, "Lord Alfred."

As all were drinking the toast, John, who was already showing signs of inebriation, raised his glass again and shouted, "To Alfred . . . the sleeping mystery!" and upturned his glass, emptying it all in one gulp.

There was stunned silence in the room. Father glared in disapproval at his eldest son while Mother bowed her head in embarrassment.

The king chose to ignore John and invited me to return to the dais. "And now, in case there's anyone here who doesn't already know this . . . ," my grandfather paused for polite laughter, "let's conclude this night's formalities with the announcement of the betrothal of Lord Alfred to the Lady Gwendolyn, daughter of Lord Godwin and Lady Margaret of the Kingdom of Lakes, grand-niece of our great friend the king of that realm."

He took my left hand and her right and joined them in front of him, then raised his glass again. "Alfred and Gwendolyn." I gave her hand a little squeeze and smiled at her, both of which she returned. Perhaps we were off to a good start. The crowd echoed the king's words, the toast was drunk, and Grandfather resumed his seat. He signaled to the musicians and the evening's entertainment began.

There were jugglers and stilt-walkers, acrobats, and a puppet show. And of course, there was dancing. Gwendolyn seemed pleased that I'm a competent dancer. When it was John's turn to partner her, I was surprised by how talkative he was. "You should've seen *my* coming-of-age celebration. Now that was *really* grand."

"I'm sure it was, Lord John."

"Lasted all night, I'm told. But then, around midnight, my mates and I all went in search of some female companionship for the rest of the evening."

He was almost certainly trying to shock her, but she didn't react or reply.

"Maybe you and I should have a little talk sometime. I could tell you things about Alfred that no one else will," he remarked.

"I suppose brothers are like sisters," she said. "They sometimes have their own secrets."

He grinned, his expression not quite menacing, yet somehow not jovial either. "Perhaps I should tell you about the night I introduced him to the pleasures of the barmaids. I think he quite enjoyed it."

She was visibly embarrassed by his crudeness. "Is that really proper conversation for polite company, Lord John?"

He laughed out loud. "Prim and proper, are we? No doubt just what my brother deserves."

I could only hope she attributed his bad behavior to an excess of wine. Otherwise, he was doing me no favors by making her uncomfortable at her very first court celebration here.

The next morning, reality hit me in the face as if I'd been slapped with a glove and challenged to a duel. Three weeks . . . so *very* little time to come to know another person, especially someone you might spend the rest of your life with. Even though I knew I wasn't inexorably committed to this marriage, I also knew how advantageous it would be to both our family and the kingdom.

Returning from my morning ride, I saw Gwendolyn and her maid descending the front steps and rushed to catch them up. "Good morning, Lady Gwendolyn. I trust you slept well?" No bowing or kissing of hands this time, for which she seemed grateful. Perhaps she, too, was ready to see what normal life might be like.

"I hope, Lord Alfred, that we can dispense with the formal address. After all, if we're to be married . . . "

"I'd like that as well." Her manner seemed easy and comfortable.

"To answer your question, I slept very well indeed. Letty and I were just going for a turn around the garden to enjoy the morning air."

"May I join you?"

She hesitated, no doubt wondering if her maid was enough of a chaperone. I watched as her hesitation turned almost immediately to resolve. "If you wish," she replied. I fell in step beside her as Letty moved to walk just behind.

"This way. The garden is at the back of the new wing of the castle. The path is just here. I hope you enjoyed yesterday as much as I did."

"It was a delightful day. And I've never seen a horse race quite like that." She laughed—a melodious sound of unbridled spontaneity that I knew I would always enjoy hearing. "That's something my mates and I devised. We compete with each other like that all the time in the fields and meadows, jumping low walls and hedges, so we thought why not do the same in the tournament?"

"I think everyone was pleased that you won."

"Oh, any one of us might have won. We're all good horsemen, so sometimes it's just a matter of luck." I wanted her to understand that I don't demand deference from my friends, regardless of my rank.

"I must apologize to you, Gwendolyn, for my brother's unseemly behavior last night. Sometimes he can be rather unpleasant."

Hesitation once again. Something she wanted to ask but was unsure of what I might think. "It seems your brother doesn't much like you."

"Sometimes he doesn't." I paused before adding, "Truth be told, most of the time he doesn't." She didn't press. Good manners seemed to be one of her assets. But she deserved to know.

"I've thought a lot about why that is," I told her. "And I've come to the conclusion that Mother is right."

"What does she think?"

"It goes back to when he was born. My uncle Harold's wife and baby died in childbirth and he hasn't remarried. Uncle Rupert's family lives at the port. My aunts all live abroad, and one of them is a nun. So when John was born, he was the only royal baby here and, as you might imagine, he got an inordinate amount of attention. Then I came along and some of that attention got diverted to me. We got along reasonably well until we were both in school together. I did well at school because I liked it; he was quite the opposite. So he began to resent the fact that I got more of our parents' approval as a result. For those years, I was nothing but a thorn in his side. Then, when he left school and started his physical training, we were no longer in competition, so he was my great friend again for a couple of years. But it didn't last."

"Do you know why?"

"He claims it's because neither I nor the sons of the nobility show him the respect and deference he thinks he's entitled to. And that may be. But I think it's really because I started getting more of

Grandfather's attention."

"Why wouldn't your grandfather do the same for both of you?"

"I asked him that once. It seems John was given chances but turned them down. Then, when he saw Grandfather take me under his wing, all the old resentments flared back up, and we've never really been friends since then. I've learned life's a lot more pleasant if I just stay out of his way."

"That must be hard, since you have no other brothers."

"It's no hardship. Samuel and Richard are like brothers to me. Phillip and Laurence are great friends as well."

"May I ask why your brother isn't married? After all, he's . . . what? . . . two years older?"

"It's not for lack of Father's trying. At one point, he'd nearly finalized a contract for John to wed Lord Devereux's niece, and the girl was brought here for them to meet before everything was signed. John took one look at her, declared she looked like a sow with the face of a sheep, and proclaimed he'd leave home and marry a farmer's daughter before he'd ever be forced to bed such a one. The girl did tend toward chubbiness, but she didn't deserve John's churlish reaction. Father knew, though, that John would follow through on his threat. So when the girl's father asked to withdraw from the contract, my father quietly agreed. I've often thought Lord Devereux may have intervened to spare my father the embarrassment of having to be the one to put a stop to things.

"It's still Father's biggest dilemma. He can't risk alienating any of our noble families . . . or even those of our neighboring kingdoms . . . by contracting for a marriage that John doesn't wholeheartedly embrace, because otherwise, my brother would just make his wife's life a misery. And because of John's place in the succession, Father can't marry him to a merchant's daughter, no matter how wealthy her family might be."

"Why hasn't your Uncle Harold remarried?"

"I really don't know. But if he had an heir, so many other problems would be solved."

We walked in silence for a few moments, but I sensed there was something else on her mind. "I've been wanting to ask," she began tentatively.

"About what?"

"That incident in the square on the day we arrived."

"What incident?"

"The one where Sir Cedric sent guards to deal with those men. I think Cedric called them 'Ranulf's sons'?"

"Oh, that. Nothing for you to worry about."

"But you and Sir Cedric both seemed quite disturbed."

"Very well, I'll tell you. But it really is nothing for you to worry about. The story dates back to when Grandfather absolved Sir Cedric of any blame in my great-grandfather's death. Sir Ranulf was a knight then . . . one of those who resented Cedric because he was in such favor with the king despite having come from a very humble background. Ranulf was certain Cedric had risen too far beyond his station. So when the wound from Cedric's arrow festered and caused the king's death, Ranulf was sure this would be his chance to be rid of Cedric once and for all. He was certain Cedric would be found guilty of regicide and executed.

"When Grandfather declared Cedric innocent of any crime, Ranulf was enraged. He swore vengeance on both Cedric and my grandfather, stormed out of the square, and deserted the knighthood; and no one saw or heard from him for years. He reappeared leading a small band of renegades that included his three sons and began terrorizing small villages and farms in the west. They never harmed anyone—just scared people out of their wits, occasionally demanded money or stole a chicken or a horse, and then rode off."

"Oh, dear! Couldn't anyone stop them?"

"Some people think Ranulf still had friends in the knighthood who were warning him when and where the patrols would be. That doesn't seem likely, though, because it takes time to send messages, and these raids were swift and unpredictable. Father thinks they were trying to draw the patrols well away from here so there wouldn't be reinforcements nearby. It almost worked. Cedric was captaining a patrol in Bauldry's domain one summer when Ranulf's band attacked at night. They killed the sentry quietly, but Ranulf made the mistake of drawing his sword to kill Cedric. The sound of it woke Cedric, and he managed to roll out of the way as Ranulf's sword came down. But that meant Cedric's own sword was now out of reach. He shouted to wake the others and they scrambled into action, fighting off the intruders, but not before Ranulf managed to inflict a rather nasty wound to Cedric's left arm. The band fled on horseback and vanished into the night by the time Cedric's men could organize a pursuit. They didn't chase far, fearing that the renegades would circle back and attack the camp again while their forces were reduced.

"They got Cedric home, and his wound healed, but he was mortified that a man had been killed on an ordinary patrol when he was in charge, so he set about resigning from the knighthood. Grandfather wouldn't hear of it. He made Sir Cedric knight commander instead. The story goes that he told Cedric 'You'll be safer here surrounded by knights, and I'll be safer with you in charge of my protection.' Cedric is not the type to refuse an honor from his king."

"Did they ever go after your grandfather?"

"Frankly, I don't know. I've heard stories they were seen once or twice shadowing the patrols he rode with, but I don't know why they wouldn't have attacked since Ranulf seemed so intent on vengeance. I've always thought it a bit of a mystery.

"Anyway, Grandfather has always arranged to keep Cedric close by. When it came time for him to retire as knight commander, Grandfather appointed him to oversee training. Then when Cedric retired from that post, Grandfather kept finding special assignments so that Cedric would always be here, surrounded by knights. It seems to have worked out to everyone's satisfaction. Well, everyone's except Ranulf's," I added with a chuckle.

"The last time I knew anything about their whereabouts was two years ago, when they were living in the highlands of the Peaks Kingdom. So you can imagine my surprise when Cedric spied the sons in the market square that day. It really is nothing for you to worry about, Gwendolyn . . . nothing to do with you or me."

She seemed to accept my reassurance, but I had no doubt she was a bit unnerved to know the renegades were so close by, still with vengeance in mind.

We had made four circuits of the garden as we were talking and had once again arrived at the path to the courtyard. It seemed she'd decided this was enough for one morning. "I've no wish to seem rude, Alfred, but I believe my mother's expecting me to join her before the midday meal."

"Then, by all means, you shouldn't be late. Perhaps we can do this again tomorrow? It's my habit to go riding every morning that the weather permits, but I'm always back about the time you met me today."

"I think I'd like that very much."

I stayed in the garden as they returned to the courtyard. I was beginning to think I liked this woman. And if we could continue to have these kinds of conversations, then perhaps we really could come to know each other well enough to be sure the marriage would be suitable. Father told me this morning that Lord Godwin had made the same arrangement with his daughter — she can back out of the contract for any reason . . . or even for no reason at all. Yet despite what our respective fathers had said, I was under no illusion that she didn't know as well as I did how much they saw this marriage as advantageous to both kingdoms — how much they wanted it to go forward. There'd been no mention of what my grandfather might think.

The following morning, Gwendolyn and Letty were already in the garden when I arrived. "It's such a lovely day," she said, as if to excuse what I might mistake for an improper excess of eagerness. "We decided to come down early and enjoy the sunshine." We started with pleasantries . . . the fine weather . . . the flowers emerging as the garden put on its spring finery . . . where I went on this morning's ride. And then I asked, "And what, my dear Gwendolyn, would you like to talk about today?"

She didn't hesitate, apparently having given this quite a bit of thought. "So now that you've come of age, what will be your role?"

I paused before answering. "May I be totally honest with you?"

"That seems the best way for us to decide if we want to be married."

"Then, to answer your question, I really don't know. I'd expected Grandfather to have given me an assignment by now, and I'm not quite sure why he hasn't."

"Perhaps right now, your assignment is to take a wife." She smiled.

"Perhaps, indeed!" I laughed. But it was a serious question. She deserved to know what her life would be like with a husband who must always serve his king but who had little prospect of ever doing anything more. "More likely, he's hoping I'll think of something on my own. But I have to admit to you, I have no grand ideas. Not even any small ones, for that matter. I do know that I'll serve him in whatever way he asks and will do the same for Uncle Harold when the time comes. Maybe that's the only role possible for royals not close to the succession. I hope that doesn't disappoint you."

The wistfulness in my tone surprised me. I'd never really considered wanting anything more than that from my life, but having said it out loud to someone trying to decide if she wanted to share that life, it seemed rather hollow. Best, perhaps, not to dwell on that, as there's little prospect of changing it. "And what, pray tell, Lady Gwendolyn," I asked with considerably greater cheerfulness, "would you like your role to be?"

"I want to be a good wife, of course, and to have children."

"How many?"

"I'm not sure. Three . . . maybe four?" Her hesitation again. Testing my reaction? I'd heard nothing with which to disagree. Then she continued. "Alfred, may I be completely honest?"

"That seems the best way . . . ," I began, and we both laughed.

"Even if I might shock you?"

"Even to that."

"I want those other things . . . a good marriage and children . . . I truly do. But Alfred, I want to *do* something. Something more than sitting with the ladies over needlework and court gossip. Oh, I know those things are necessary at court. But my tutors opened my eyes to how much more there is in the world than just sewing and dancing. I want to do something that's important."

"Do you know what that might be?"

"No more than you." She paused and walked to the side of the path to examine a rose bush covered in buds about to burst into flower. Whatever she was thinking seemed to be of grave concern. At long last she turned back to me and looked directly into my eyes, apparently resolved on a course of action. "What I do know," she said with conviction, "is that I want a husband who will not forbid it to me when I find it."

We walked on in silence. This, then, must have been the reason my father left the decision in my hands. The wife he'd chosen for me was a woman who knew her own mind, who wanted more for herself than simply making a comfortable life for her husband, who wanted a role to play, who wanted to use her mind and not just use her body to bear children. Someone not content with trivialities who wanted to be a partner in this marriage. And Godwin presumably knew that his daughter would be content with nothing less. Up ahead I spied an early-blooming rose bush covered in deep red flowers. The red rose. Gwendolyn's own symbol. I used my dagger to cut a blossom and remove the thorns, then turned to tuck it into her curls. Taking her hands in mine, I looked deep into her eyes. "Would it surprise you to know that I'm not shocked . . . that I think I'm actually rather pleased? You see, I've read of Roman women who had more influence than many people know about. And Grandfather has always been interested in new ideas, so I've grown up with that notion. We could figure it out together when the time comes if that's alright with you?"

It was as if she'd been holding her breath the entire time and could now exhale once again. In her hands, I could feel the tension leave her body. And her smile returned, radiant as the sun. "That's very alright with me." We had cleared, I remember thinking, the biggest hurdle in our courtship, and now our conversations could be about planning for the future rather than worrying about what might get in the way. I understood then that I was beginning to fall in love.

And then it rained for five days. Just when I was so looking forward to more walks in the garden. We saw each other at meals. My mates and I joined Gwendolyn and her sisters in Mother's sitting room for afternoon chats. But it was nothing like the intimate conversations we'd started those two mornings in the garden. I knew real life was like this, but that did little to assuage my disappointment. Nor hers, I think.

Then, on the fifth morning, with the rain still pouring down, I had an inspiration. "Osbert, why don't you go to Lady Gwendolyn and ask if she and Letty would be so good as to join me in the library?"

"I be thinking mayhap that be a good idea, m'lord. Miss Letty say her lady be not so happy with the rain." And he was off on his errand.

I was waiting when they arrived and watched in silence as she walked slowly around the room, reading some of the titles, now and then reaching out to touch a particularly beautiful binding. When she'd made a complete circuit of the room, she turned to me with absolute joy on her face. "Father had told me about this place, but it's more impressive than anything I ever imagined. More books than I've ever seen in my entire life."

"I was hoping you'd like it."

"Like it? I can't even begin to take it all in. It's a treasure. One could spend a lifetime reading all these."

"And that would be a lifetime well spent, I think."

"For once, I wish my Latin were better. I always preferred mathematics . . . I convinced my tutor to teach me geometry rather than more Latin because I fancied becoming an architect." She looked at me a bit sheepishly, thinking, I suppose, that such a notion for a woman must seem ridiculous. I merely smiled, so she continued, "But now I fear I'll miss out on getting to know what's inside some of these beautiful volumes." I suddenly realized she was speaking as if it were a certainty she'd be spending the rest of her life here.

"We could read them together." I paused as she blushed ever so slightly. "Here, let me show you some of my favorites." I took her around the room pointing out books that my grandfather had copied as a young man, rare volumes that exist in only one or two places in the entire world, a small book of verses that I myself copied when I was very young. I showed her two beautiful illuminated manuscripts. "Created by the monks of our monastery. They're among my grandfather's very favorites."

"I think these books must also be your friends."

"Some of my happiest hours have been spent in this room."

"Since I first learned," she said, "I've always delighted in reading. I've read my father's books so many times that I can practically recite them from memory." And now I knew we shared another passion in common.

"Grandfather allows everyone at court access to the library. If you want to take a book to your room, you need only write your name on one of these little wooden sticks and put it in the place of the book. It's an ingenious system, because then you know exactly where to place the book when you return it."

"You mean . . . even now . . . I could . . . "

"Even now . . . and every day that you live under this roof."

And then, a week later, it seemed as if it would all fall apart. The weather had finally improved so we'd resumed our garden walks. Gwendolyn had begun allowing me to hold her hand as we walked, which I took as a sign that, she, too, was falling in love. We said goodbye that morning as usual, and I returned to my apartment to speak with Osbert before joining my father and Lord Godwin for the midday meal. Making my way to my parents' apartment, I spied Gwendolyn rushing down the crossing corridor, pulling Letty behind her. "Wait," I called out, to no avail, so I quickened my pace to catch them up.

"M'lady, stop," Letty was pleading as I arrived. "It be only Lord Alfred." Gwendolyn turned toward me, tears streaming down her face, the fear in her eyes absolutely palpable.

"What's wrong?" I asked.

"No, Alfred. Not now. I can't do this. I can't. It wasn't meant to be." I put a hand on one of her shoulders and raised her chin to look at me, but she kept her eyes downcast, tears still flowing. "No, Alfred. Let me go."

"Letty, what's happened?"

"It were Lord John, m'lord. He treat m'lady ever so shameful."

"Gwendolyn, look at me." She complied reluctantly. "Now, let's find a place we can talk. Letty, do you have a handkerchief for your mistress?"

"Aye, m'lord." Gwendolyn took it and dabbed at her tears.

"Now give me your hand. We're going to walk to the library . . . it's just around the corner and no one will bother us there." What could have happened that this woman who is so strong-willed could be reduced to such abject terror? I said nothing more until we were safely inside the library with the door closed. "Letty, let's get your mistress settled on the couch in front of the hearth." I took a chair nearby and waited patiently while Letty helped Gwendolyn get control of herself.

"Now tell me exactly what happened."

"I can't, Alfred. I can't do this."

Letty purred and fretted over her, patting her back and holding her hand. "Best you tell him, m'lady. It won't be so bad once he knows. I know you not be afraid of Lord Alfred."

Finally, she decided. "We were coming back from the garden . . . climbing the stairs." I saw Letty squeeze her hand in encouragement. "Suddenly he was there, on the step above me, blocking our way." She paused.

"Tell m'lord what he said," Letty encouraged.

"He was sneering . . . like a wolf salivating over its prey . . . and the expression in his eyes." Letty squeezed her hand again. "And he said, 'Well, well, well. If it isn't my brother's bride-to-be. They give him a rose from the garden and offer me a cow from the fields. That doesn't seem right somehow.' I stepped to the side, intending to go around, and he moved to block my way. 'Maybe I should claim the rose for myself,' he said."

"He look m'lady up and down," Letty added. "Like if he be trying to work out what she look like without any clothes. Then he touch her hair and her cheek."

Gwendolyn's fear seemed to be changing to anger. "He caressed my cheek and said, 'Such a delicate rose. Such a jewel to be treasured.'

Then he grinned . . . oh, such an evil grin . . . before he said, 'Such a treasure to explore . . . one . . . little . . . bit . . . at a time,' all the while stroking my cheek and twirling bits of my hair around his finger.

"Then he laughed and stepped aside. I grabbed Letty's hand and ran up the stairs, leaving him laughing behind us. I was on my way to my parents' chamber when you waylaid us."

I took her hand. "Tell me . . . please . . . that he didn't actually harm you." My tone was as cold as steel. "If he hurt you in any way, I'll . . ."

She raised her hand to silence me. "He didn't hurt me, Alfred. But I was terrified." I went to a cabinet in the corner of the room, filled a small glass, and gave it to her. "Drink this." As she examined the amber liquid, I added, "Brandy. It will soothe your nerves."

She took a sip. "Alfred, I don't know if I can live with that kind of fear hanging over my head all the time."

I poured my own glass of brandy and sat beside her. "And you shouldn't. And you won't. And I'll make certain he never threatens you again."

"But what can you do, Alfred? You said yourself he's unpredictable . . . your friend one day, resenting you the next. You can't send him away . . . this is his home . . . so he'll always be here . . . lurking."

"Maybe I can't send him away, but Grandfather can. Some assignment far away from here. Maybe the knighthood."

"You can't go whining to your grandfather every time John does something he shouldn't."

"I never have." I downed my brandy in a single gulp. "But maybe it's time I did." I put my glass down on the table with a firmness that matched my resolution.

"Don't do something foolish, Alfred. I can*not* come between you and your family. They would grow to dislike me, and I'd always be uneasy with them. We could never be happy."

I dropped to one knee in front of her, took both her hands in mine, and looked deep into her eyes. "Don't you see, Gwen? I want *you* to be my family. I'll do whatever it takes . . . even if that means fighting my brother . . . or embarrassing myself with the king . . . for you to feel safe."

Her eyes brimmed with tears once more.

I repeated in almost a whisper. "I want *you* to be my family, Gwen. I want *you* to be my wife."

Letty put an arm around her shoulder. She took another sip of brandy then stared into the glass, deep in thought. When she set the glass down, it was as if she'd reached a decision. She shrugged free of Letty's embrace and reached out a hand to touch my cheek. "I want *you* to be *my* family, too, Alfred."

I stood, lifted her to her feet, and kissed her on the forehead. "Now . . . if John ever threatens you again, promise me you'll shout for the guards. They may not always be where you can see them, but they're always within the sound of a raised voice. You, too, Letty. Don't even think twice. Promise me."

"Aye, m'lord," Letty stood and bobbed a little curtsey.

"I promise as well, Alfred," said Gwen. "And I promised your mother I'd join her for the midday meal, so I'd best start making my way there."

"Let me walk with you."

"Oh, I'm sure John's long gone by now."

"And I'm not taking any chances."

The next day we resumed our garden walks. I worried that she may have had second thoughts, but there was no sign of it as she started the conversation. "I remember on that first day that Sir Cedric introduced you as Patron of the Royal Kennel. That's not a role we have in our land."

"I think it's something my grandfather invented for me," I laughed. "But if you'd like to see what it's all about, we can ride to the monastery for a visit." Then, remembering we needed a chaperone, I added, "I think your father might enjoy seeing this as well."

"Before you go find him, I have something else that may shock you."

"Another surprise?"

"You see, it's my habit when I ride for other than formal occasions to ride astride, like a man. I have special skirts made for this purpose."

"What a wonderful idea! Perhaps I'll challenge you to a race."

She was utterly enthralled with the dogs themselves and seemed genuinely interested in my task of creating a long-term purpose for the kennel. I recall thinking even then that this might one day become the role she was looking for beyond motherhood.

Two days later Gwen celebrated her eighteenth birthday. To honor the occasion, Grandfather invited us and our parents to dine with him in his private chambers. At the end of the meal, he brought up what must have been his purpose in inviting us. "So, do either of you," he looked first at Gwen and then at me, "know of any reason why I should tell the bishop he can change his plans for a week hence?"

We looked at each other for a long time and then replied almost simultaneously, "None that we know of, sir," though Gwen said "Your Grace."

The king beamed. "That is most welcome news. For us as a family, dear Gwendolyn, and for the kingdom."

"If it please Your Grace, my closest family call me Gwen."

"If it's all the same to you, my dear, I prefer to call you Gwendolyn. It suits you well. Besides, whatever I call you will be imitated by all and sundry, and it's my understanding that you prefer your full name outside your close family."

"That's true, Your Grace."

"One thing I *will* request, however. Within our family, we save the formalities of address for public occasions. Perhaps you could see your way clear to think of me less as 'Your Grace' and more as your grandfather-in-law."

"As you wish, sir. That would please me very much indeed."

"Very well then. Now that that's settled, I have a birthday gift for you." He stepped to a sideboard and returned with a small carved box that he placed in front of her on the table. She opened it slowly and carefully. Inside the box, on a lining of purple velvet, was a beautiful strand of pearls.

"They belonged to my late wife, who received them from her mother on her wedding day. In her will, she expressly designated them for Alfred's future bride, should I deem her worthy and assuming she agreed to maintain the tradition of passing them on to a future generation."

He took the pearls from the box and clasped them around Gwen's neck. "I shall wear them with pride and humility, sir. And I shall happily honor your wife's memory by ensuring that the next recipient is a daughter of your house."

From Lord Godwin and Lady Margaret, silver earrings. My gift, a silver bracelet. From my parents, a beautiful silk scarf.

Father showed us the new banner we would receive on the occasion of our marriage. It combines our symbols, and we're allowed to use the royal family coronet. I was happy and proud, and it seemed as if Gwen felt the same.

I scarcely remember the details of our wedding. It being the first royal wedding in more than two decades, Grandfather was determined to make it a splendid one. His fellow kings from the Lakes and Peaks came as did all the nobles from this kingdom and the ambassadors from other lands. I do remember when I caught sight of Gwen, a golden vision in silk and lace, framed in the arch of the nave as she took her father's arm to walk up the aisle, the sapphires she wore perfectly matching her eyes. I recall that the banquet was even more elaborate than for my coming-of-age celebration, but I remember nothing of what was served. I'm told the dancing and entertainment went on long after the ritual of putting the newly married couple to bed, when my mates, Gwen's sisters, and my female cousins escorted us to our apartment, bade us goodnight, and locked the door from the outside.

At last they were gone and we were truly alone for the first time. I took Gwen in my arms and kissed her deeply and passionately. She didn't shy away. Then I stepped back, took both her hands in mine, surveyed her from head to toe, and kissed her gently on the forehead. "I'll retire until you're ready." I went into my dressing room and shut the door.

"I be thinking ye be a right lucky man, m'lord," said Osbert as he helped me out of my boots.

"In what way, Osbert?"

"Well, m'lady be ever so pretty . . . mayhap the prettiest lady I ever did see."

"I cannot disagree with you there."

"Ye needs to be special gentle with her this night, sir, so's she not be frightened, see?"

His sudden compulsion to dispense fatherly advice brought a smile to my face. "I can promise you, Osbert, you need have no concern on that score." And then I was struck by a very peculiar notion. I actually had John to thank for my lack of anxiety about being with a woman that night. The thought made me chuckle out loud.

"What be so funny, m'lord?"

Thanks to my brother and his barmaids, the feelings I had that night were of love and lust and excitement and anticipation and joy and an almost desperate desire to be pleasing to her and to please her so that she never shied away from the pleasures of the bed chamber. And what was that, I asked myself, but just a different kind of anxiety? I chuckled aloud again.

"M'lord?" Osbert was thoroughly confused.

"Nothing to worry your head about, Osbert. I was just remembering something that happened long before we met."

A soft knock on the door was Letty's signal that her mistress was ready. Apparently suffering from his own anxiety, Osbert fussed over me yet again, straightening my night shirt for the third or fourth time then stepping back to appraise his handiwork. "If ye not be needing aught else, m'lord, Letty and me be staying in the servants hall this night."

"I think we'll be fine, Osbert. After all, we both wanted this marriage." He looked around the room a final time before leaving through his private doorway into the corridor.

I opened the dressing room door to find Gwen standing at a window, looking out into the courtyard. She wore a beautiful nightdress, all silk and lace and tiny beads, and her hair hung loose around her shoulders and down her back. The mere sight of her would be enough to arouse any man. I was a lucky one indeed. I crossed the room slowly and embraced her, then took her hands and held her at arm's length. "You are an absolute vision of loveliness."

"And you're the second person to tell me that this night."

I looked at her quizzically. "Oh?"

"The other being Letty." She smiled.

"Thank goodness! I wouldn't have wanted a rival on my wedding night."

I picked her up and carried her to the bed. Her scent was fresh and clean, with a hint of rosewater, which only served to heighten my arousal. Setting her down, I fingered the lace at the neck of her nightdress. "Perhaps we shouldn't risk damaging this. I'd very much like to see you in it many more times." I helped her out of the nightdress and pulled the covers over her nakedness before walking around the bed, removing my nightshirt, and slipping into bed beside her.

I kissed her and caressed her hair then let my hand slide down to touch her breasts. Her skin was soft and warm and she reached out to caress my face. "If you're nervous, my darling, we can take this as slowly as you like," I told her.

"I know what to expect, Alfred. Mother said it can be quite wonderful with a man who's kind and loving. But I don't know what to do, so you'll have to be my guide. Just please don't do anything to make me dread being with you for the rest of our lives."

I took her hand from my face and brought its palm to my lips. Then I kissed her forehead, her eyelids, and finally her lips before saying, "That's something I'd never want to do." I propped myself up on one elbow and gazed into her eyes. "Besides, Osbert gave me strict instructions that I must be especially gentle with you tonight."

She laughed softly. "And Letty assured me more than once that she knew you would be exactly that." She wriggled her body closer to mine and I held her tightly. There's no doubt she could feel the stiffness in my crotch, but she didn't shy away.

"I'm told," I whispered, "that the first time it may hurt you a bit.

I'm sorry for that, but I understand it doesn't last long and that it's only the first time."

"Then perhaps," she whispered back, "we should get that behind us."

"Tell me if you want me to stop." As I began exploring her body, slowly moving ever downward, she seemed to enjoy my caresses. When I moved a hand between her legs, she parted them slightly, as if in invitation. My anticipation grew.

I moved on top of her and she stroked my chest. When I entered her, she gasped in astonishment. "Are you alright?"

"I think I shall be quite alright," she whispered in reply.

When it was over, I lay quietly on top of her for some minutes, savoring the utter delight of her. Then I rolled onto my back and sleep overtook me.

Later in the night we explored each other again. This time, she, too, was spent, and we both fell quickly asleep.

When I woke again, the draperies had been parted slightly to let in some morning light. I donned my nightshirt and sat before the hearth. When I heard Gwen stir, I took her the robe Letty had left on the chair. "Apparently," I chuckled, pointing to the tray of food on the table, "someone thought we might be in need of nourishment this morning." Letty must have come in quietly while we were still asleep to leave a tray of bread, butter and jam, and some cider.

"I must admit," she said, "that I'm rather more hungry than usual this morning." She poured cider into the two cups, and we enjoyed what turned out to be a most welcome breakfast.

"I thought today we might go riding," I said, "if that's agreeable to you."

"That sounds delightful! Perhaps you can show me some more of your old haunts now that we can go about without so many chaperones."

"My mates want to fête us this evening . . . drinks and supper at the tavern in the town. What do you think?"

"I think I'd like it very much. It's market day, right? Perhaps if we go to town a bit early, we can wander around the stalls. It would be nice to be among the town folk."

"Are you sure you haven't been taking lessons from my grandfather?"

"Why do you ask?"

"I remember his advice to me long ago . . . 'It's always a good thing to go about among the people so they learn to know and trust you. You never know when you might need to rely on their love and support, so build it well before ever the need should arise.'"

"Then we should follow his advice together every chance we get. Now I suppose we must let the day and the real world back into our pleasant little cocoon."

Not long after Gwen and I were married, John announced that he was entering the knighthood. Such a departure from his usual devil-may-care attitude came as quite a surprise. "He didn't have much choice," my father said when I asked about the sudden change. "I'd lost whatever control I once had over him, so your grandfather intervened. Told him he could start acting like a responsible member of the royal family or suffer the consequences.

"Your brother was insolent, as usual. I believe his exact words to your grandfather were, 'And if I don't, there's really not much you can do about it, is there?'

"Father was magnificent. 'Oh, there's quite a lot I can do about it,' he said. 'I can disinherit you and ensure that you never get a single coin of inheritance from me directly or through your father or his brothers. I can revoke your privilege to live here in the castle, and you'll have to fend for yourself in whatever way you can. I can even remove you from the order of succession. In case you've forgotten, let me remind you that our law provides that a king's will may specify the succession for two generations following him. Only the absence of such a specification in a king's will sets the stage for what we've come to think of as the normal order. I can do all of that and more. And believe me, I will.' He paused to let it sink in.

"Then he went on, 'So you have a choice. Starting this day you can begin to act like a responsible adult and give the people of this realm a reason to respect you as a member of this family, or you can start to see your present and future privileges withdrawn systematically.'

"He seems to have gotten John's attention at last. Frankly, we're both rather relieved that he chose the knighthood because neither of us could think of an assignment to give him that he wouldn't make a dog's breakfast of."

"Why didn't Grandfather just disinherit him outright?"

"I asked him that. He seems to think that the threat of removing him from the succession is the last motivation we have to exert any control over your brother's behavior. It's a risk, I know, so we just have to hope Harold finds a wife and gets himself an heir."

Having John out of the castle, often away on one assignment or another, proved a boon for everyone. No one missed the disruption that always seemed to follow in his wake.

Samuel, too, joined the knighthood. Him, I missed when he was off on patrol.

Phillip was away from time to time, too, working with his father on trade missions. But it seemed there was trouble brewing on that front. Father and I were both at the Council meeting when it was discussed. Father held the family seat on the Council at that time; I was there at Grandfather's invitation—something he'd been doing more frequently in those days.

"Ranulf and his sons are growing bolder," Thorssen began. "Not only are they showing themselves more frequently among the Peaksmen, but they've begun stalking our trade. Captain Norris led the last two expeditions." He turned to a young knight seated beside him. "Norris?"

"Your Grace . . . your lordships . . . it's happened on both trips. The first time, they simply shadowed us along the lower reaches of the hills as we traveled from our border to the Peaks castle. There were only the four of them, but they made sure we could see them the whole way . . . made sure we knew they were there.

"On this last trip, they were more aggressive. We started seeing them in the foothills just before we crossed the border. So when we made camp for the night of the beacons, I doubled the sentries. That meant my men didn't get much sleep that night, but it seemed safer. Good thing I did, too, because we discovered one of them skulking around the picket lines among the horses. When the sentry raised the alarm, the intruder fled before we could catch him. And the next day, there they were again, shadowing the entire rest of our journey to the castle."

"It's rather curious," Thorssen added. "They shadow the expedition on the trip *to* the Peaks castle, but you've not seen them on the return journey, right, Norris?"

"Right, my lord. But I still double the sentries until we're well inside our border. Don't want my men caught unawares."

"Captain, what's your assessment of what they're up to?" asked Lord Montfort.

"I'm not rightly sure, your lordship. At first, I thought they were just looking for an opportunity to attack us and kill some of my men. The part I can't make sense of, though, is what Lord Thorssen said. Why don't they follow us out? Maybe it's actually our Peaks escort they're after, since the escort doesn't accompany us on the return trip. But then with the episode in the picket lines on the last trip, I've begun to wonder if maybe they're after our horses. Whatever they're up to, it's worrisome. I've asked the commander to double the size of my troop for the next trip so we can be prepared for whatever they try next."

"Might be a good idea," Meriden chimed in, "to send a troop to hunt them down. They need to be brought to justice."

"I take your point, Meriden," said Grandfather, "but until they commit a crime, there's really no justice to administer. Captain, what were the trade goods of the last two expeditions?"

"Both were grain, Your Grace. We returned with some bows on the first trip and with a dog for Lord Alfred's kennel on the last trip."

"So I'm coming to the conclusion, gentlemen," said Thorssen, "that it's either horses or grain they're after. I can see why they'd want horses. I'm really not sure why they'd want the grain, since there's no famine in the Peaks kingdom and no reason for them to be hungry."

There was silence around the table as Thorssen dismissed Sir Norris. Finally, Montfort spoke.

"What if Ranulf wants not just a sack of grain for himself, but the whole shipment? And every shipment he can get his hands on. What if his intent is to become the supplier of grain for the people in the highlands where he's been living? To turn their loyalty away from the Peaks king—who won't have the grain to distribute—and toward himself. What if he's trying to sow disruption within the Peaks kingdom, build a following, and either set himself up in power there or create enough of a power base from which to pursue his vengeance? What if he's trying to get the Peaks kingdom to turn on us? Infiltrating his gang into a battlefield would be a good way to get close enough that killing our king would be possible."

For a moment, the silence returned. Then the room broke into a cacophony of voices, each trying to be heard over its neighbor, some claiming the idea was preposterous and others starting to speculate on what could happen and what we should do about it.

Devereux brought order back to the room. "Gentlemen . . . please." He paused until the room was quiet again. "What Montfort postulated rings true for me. We all know Ranulf has been looking for an opportunity to render his own personal version of vengeance. I think we should consider our actions with that in mind."

In the end, most were aligned with Devereux. Meriden was just a little too eager to send a hunting party after Ranulf's band, but thankfully wasn't in one of his more strident moods.

"Very well," said my grandfather. "I'll charge our ambassador to the Peaks to discuss with their King how we address the threat. Thorssen, you and the knight commander draw up your own plan. When our ambassador returns, we'll combine the ideas and proceed. Commander, can you have a courier ready to ride tomorrow morning with messages for Lord Peveril and the Peaks king?"

"Of course, Sire."

"Very well. The letters will be ready at dawn."

It was almost a year to the day after our wedding that my grandfather summoned me to meet him in the library. I arrived well before the appointed time, knowing how much he appreciates promptness, but his squire admitted me immediately. "Lord Alfred, Sire."

My grandfather smiled. "You are one of the few, Alfred, whom I know will always be early. Please, sit . . . we've much to discuss. There's something I need your help with, but it means you'll be away for a considerable period of time. I've delayed getting you involved while you were newly married. You and Gwendolyn needed the time together to make your marriage strong. But it's been a year, so it's time to resume your royal duties."

"What is it you have in mind?"

"Actually, there are two things. One is to help Harold with the reservoir project. The other is a personal favor to me.

"Harold is concerned about maintaining the water levels in years when the rainfall is low—the years when we'll be releasing water for irrigation. He thinks there must have been a source for the old lake but hasn't had the time to discover it. I'm sure you could help him there."

"I'm certainly willing to try."

"It's my opinion, however, that there's an even more serious risk in the overall plan that Harold hasn't thought through. I won't prejudice your thinking with my suspicions. Evaluate the plan, and then we can compare our views. If my concerns are ill-founded, then I'll be relieved. If not, we must take steps to mitigate the problem."

"Can you at least give me a starting place?"

"I'll say only that I think it's connected to the years of low rainfall.

Get Harold to explain his vision to you, and I think you'll have the starting point you need."

"Very well. When do you want me to begin?"

"The sooner the better. To be precise, I'd like you to be on site within the fortnight. And that's related to the personal favor.

"I've assigned a knight there — one Sir Ronan Grai. I need you to make yourself known to him and to be sure you know the faces of both him and his squire. And I need you to accomplish this without drawing anyone's attention to what you're doing. At some point, either Sir Ronan or his squire will approach you with a message to be delivered to me. The circumstances may not be what you expect. I ask only that you get the message to me with the utmost dispatch and with no chance that it could be intercepted should the messenger be waylaid or captured. You're to take no other action on your own initiative."

"Am I to know any more about the reason for this message or why it's so important?"

"I'm afraid not, Alfred. I must ask you to simply accept that it's of the utmost importance and to trust me in this matter. You must also keep this part of your mission entirely secret. Tell absolutely no one about it. In due course, things will become clear."

"Of course I trust you, Grandfather," I said, lapsing into a familiarity that we don't use often but that I knew would convey to him the depth of my trust. "Is there anything else?"

"That's actually quite a lot, Alfred, especially when combined with the fact that I'm asking you to be away from Gwendolyn for a month or more."

That night, propped up on pillows in the bed, I told Gwen of my new assignment — everything, that is, except the part about the mysterious message. I remember feeling a pang of guilt at not sharing that with her as well, but my grandfather was quite specific.

"He's right, you know," she said, snuggling closer and laying her head on my chest.

"About what?"

"About the extraordinary time we've had to solidify our marriage.

That doesn't often happen in royal families, you know."

"Perhaps, but I'm not exactly near the top of the succession," I chuckled. "Tomorrow I'll get Osbert to start organizing what we'll need to be away. But for now," I added, snuggling down under the covers with her, "there are much more pleasant things I'd rather do." And we made love as passionately as if this were the eve of my departure.

I woke in the morning when Gwen gave me a soft kiss on the forehead just before slipping out of bed to start her morning toilette. Slowly coming fully awake, I relished the memory of last night's lovemaking. I'm a lucky man. Gwen is as ardent in bed as I am. My father taught me how to love and cherish a woman; but he also warned me that some women view sex as an obligation to be discharged solely for the purpose of producing children. In my opinion, the church and brutish men have collectively given rise to that view—and far too many women have passed it down to their daughters as absolute gospel. Thankfully, Gwen seems not to be thus tainted.

I knew from observing my parents how rewarding a marriage can be when it's a shared partnership in all things. We seemed well on our way to having the same kind of marriage—already we were both lovers and best friends.

Reluctantly, I put my musings aside, turned back the covers, and emerged from my cocoon. Osbert had my clothes ready organized, as always, and as he helped me to dress, I told him of our upcoming mission. "You might want to include some winter gear among what we take. I'm not sure how long we'll be gone, and you know how a cold snap can suddenly rise up from nowhere in the early autumn."

"Right, m'lord. And I be talking to the squires who go with the supply missions to find out what sort of permanent camp there be and how much be still tents and campfires."

"I'll leave it in your capable hands, Osbert, and put my mind to other things," I gave him a hearty slap on the shoulder and headed out for my morning ride.

The day of our departure came all too soon, especially after what

Gwen revealed the night before. "I'm fairly certain I'm with child," she announced as we were finishing our supper. "So you must be sure to complete your assignment in time to be back here for its birth."

I almost choked on the swallow of wine in my mouth, so unexpected was this. "I . . . uh . . . When? . . . How soon?" I stammered, completely at a loss for words.

She smiled with amusement. "Calm down. It's not completely certain, but I've consulted your mother and the midwife, and they both say all the signs are there. Anyway, it won't be for several months yet. I just wanted you to know before you left."

"I'm . . . delighted . . . overjoyed, in fact. What do I need to do?"

"Nothing now, silly. Just do a marvelous job helping Harold, finish as soon as you can, and come back home. There'll be plenty of time then to talk about things like names and such."

"When are you planning to tell the rest of the family . . . and your parents, for that matter? Can I tell anyone?"

"Let's keep it our little secret for two or three more weeks, until I'm absolutely sure. Then we can tell the world."

"You'll write to me as soon as you're sure?"

"No, I think I'll write to the King of Lakes and tell him he's about to become a great-granduncle," she said with a straight face, waiting for me to react. After a second, I realized she was teasing and smiled. "Of course I'll write to you, you ninny," she laughed.

I took her in my arms and carried her to the bed, where I smothered her with kisses. Suddenly I stopped, sat up, and looked at her lying there.

"Can we . . . ?"

"Why not?" she asked. "Why should tonight be any different from last night or the night before?"

"I don't know. This is all new territory for me, so you'll have to be my guide."

"It's new for me, too, but nothing women haven't been doing for centuries. We'll be just fine figuring it out together."

That was all the assurance I needed to resume my caresses. We made love with extraordinary passion. And then, in the middle of the night, we both woke and made love again, slowly and tenderly.

Dawn arrived too soon. I tried to slip out of bed quietly and let Gwen sleep, but she was alert at the first sign of stirring on my part. "You don't think I'd let you leave without being there to see you off, do you?" So we both arose and began preparing for our very different days.

Once dressed, I returned to our chamber to find Gwen ready and a small breakfast on the table. "I had Letty bring this up. You have a long day in the saddle ahead of you, and it seemed like starting out with some sustenance might be a good idea."

Osbert had made arrangements for most of our gear to go on the wagons with the supply patrol that left two days ago. With only our own mounts and what we carried in our packs, we were able to travel faster. Not for the first time I reminded myself what a resourceful chap Osbert is and how much I depend on him.

We arrived at the first village on the Great Trunk Road as the sun was starting to lower in the west, so we decided to take advantage of the inn and have a nice hot meal and a comfortable night's sleep. The next night, we camped just past where the road branches off to go toward Ernle Manor and the Territories. By mid-morning of the third day, we'd caught up to the supply patrol and joined them for the rest of the journey. As we fell in behind the second pair of knights in the train, I realized that one of them was John. "Well, well, well," he just couldn't keep a tone of superiority out of his voice. "If it isn't the sleeping lion himself. What brings you here, Brother?"

"Assignment by the king," I replied.

"And of course he couldn't have asked me to do it since I was coming this way anyway." Would he never shed his insolence?

"Maybe he thought you had other duties." I tried to mollify him. The captain, I observed, was taking note of the exchange.

"Oh, very well," his usual retort when he can't think of anything else. "Fall in and make the best of it. It'll be nearing nightfall by the time we arrive."

And on that score, he proved correct. By the time we found our lodgings, attended the horses, and ate a bit of supper, it was too late to do more than have Osbert inform Uncle Harold's squire that we'd arrived and that I'd see him the following day.

We were assigned to a large tent with the other knights of the supply patrol. Without being asked, Osbert chose a spot for us in a far corner, as distant from John as feasible. John seemed no more eager to associate with me. After a long day in the saddle, the tent was soon quiet with only the occasional soft snoring of exhausted men.

I woke to the sounds of the knights collecting their gear. As I reached for my boots, Osbert returned from whatever errand he'd been on.

"Everything be here, m'lord. We be sharing the hut with Captain Arnald. Lord Harold be wanting to see ye as soon as ye be ready."

"Well done, Osbert. Lead the way."

"Aye, m'lord."

Emerging into the bright sunlight, I assessed our surroundings. Something of a basin, surrounded on three sides by hills. In the flats and on the lower slopes, small buildings and tents. The buildings, Osbert said, housed the senior knights and craftsmen assigned to the project and provided storage for tools and supplies. The tents housed the laborers and transients like the supply patrol. A larger tent in an area shaded by trees served as a dining hall, where everyone, even including Harold, took their meals. He'd clearly been industrious learning the layout and routine of the camp, which was already abuzz with activity. New supplies being unloaded. Masons at work on the dam, which seemed surprisingly near completion. Laborers mixing mortar and hauling stones. I could smell the aromas of food being prepared over the kitchen fires. "It be hard work," said Osbert, "so there always be food to keep up men's strength."

We approached two small buildings near the south end of the dam. "The one on the right be where we be living, with Captain Arnald," Osbert informed me. "There on the left be Lord Harold's quarters. I be leaving ye here then, m'lord, and go see to our gear." And he was on his way almost before I could utter a thank you.

Though the door to Harold's quarters was open, I knocked on the frame and waited to be invited in. A voice from inside said "Come," and I entered to see two men poring over drawings spread on a small table. Harold looked up briefly. "Ah, Alfred. Welcome. Find a chair. I'll be with you in a moment." And he returned to the discussion of the drawings.

After a few minutes, he stood and said, "I think that's it, Ronan. Go ahead with those final changes." The other man began gathering up the drawings in preparation to leave when Harold added, "Alfred, meet Sir Ronan Grai, an engineering genius who's helped me work out the final details on the sluice gates. Ronan, my nephew, Lord Alfred."

We nodded and mumbled greetings and Ronan went on his way. One step in my secret mission achieved far more easily than I'd expected.

Harold shook my hand and clapped me heartily on the back. "Alfred, my boy, what a welcome sight you are. Father said he'd be sending you out to help, but I didn't know you'd be here so soon. There's so much I want to finish before winter, and we're well on our way; with your help, we should just about make it."

"Grandfather said you wanted to locate the old source of water for the lake."

"Here, sit." He gestured toward the table. "Let me show you. How much do you know about what we're doing here?"

"Just the broad picture."

"Then let me fill in the details. I first came across this place on a hunting trip with Ernle. We were following a herd of deer, and they came down here to drink from the pool in this depression. The rubble on the open side was enough to trap rainfall, and the deer had found a perfect watering spot. At the time, I thought it looked as if there'd once been more of a lake here but thought no more about it until your grandfather mentioned his idea of providing a source of water for the farmers and the flocks in years of scarce rainfall. I remembered this place and came back to assess is more fully. There were hewn stones and evidence of masonry amid the rubble, and I was convinced there had once been some sort of dam here forming a lake. I've been working on the assumption that it was a Roman structure. The cutting of the stones was clearly done by master craftsmen.

"I've no idea if it was intentionally destroyed or just deteriorated from years of neglect, but I'm rather inclined to the latter view, because we've been able to salvage and use almost all the original stones in the new dam. That's why we've been able to complete the new structure so quickly."

My uncle's enthusiasm for his project was evident in the excitement in his voice. "The plan is that water from the lake will be channeled into two major canals that run from here through the north and south portions of the kingdom, south of the river," he continued. "They'll eventually converge and rejoin the river beyond the port. In years of low rainfall, we can open the sluice gates, letting water into the canals, and the farmers, herdsmen, and land owners can draw the water they need into trenches they'll create. The problem I haven't solved is how to keep the lake replenished in the absence of sufficient rainfall. We need to find what the original source was for the Roman lake." Throughout this lengthy explanation, he was continuously pointing out features on the map. Then he paused for a moment to let me take it all in.

"There are three shallow gullies – here, here, and here –" again pointing on the map, "that look like they might be dry creek beds running into the depression from the west. I explored the southernmost one and found it disappeared about an hour's walk up the hillside. But I haven't had time to explore either of the other two, and that's where I could use your help."

"Osbert and I can start in the morning. Do you have any preference for which one we explore first?"

"Start with the middle one. It seems to be wider and deeper than the other. I don't want the two of you going alone, though. We've had no problems with animals or intruders since we've been here, but I don't want to take any unnecessary chances. Check with the captain and get two other men to go along with you. And don't do anything foolish."

"That would be John doing foolish things, Uncle Harold, not me."

We both chuckled at the truth of that remark. "Right then. I'll be off and make arrangements to go exploring."

"Happy hunting, Alfred. Bring me back some good news."

Arnald assigned me two squires—one, his own—for our little venture. When I protested, he laughed. "Don't concern yourself about that, Lord Alfred. Our squires are always off on some errand or another—trips into the town for fresh food on market days . . . carrying messages to the castle with progress reports, lists of what's needed in the next supply train, letters to families . . . hunting parties for fresh meat. We knights have learned to share and find it no inconvenience. After all, we don't have fancy parades or tournaments to prepare for up here in the hills."

"Then when we return, Osbert and I will join in your scheme if you'll allow us." I've never forgotten my grandfather's admonition that a king needs to build the respect and trust of those he governs. I extend that idea to all royals, no matter how unlikely that one should ever become king.

"We'd be quite pleased, my lord." I could tell from his tone and expression that my gesture was both unexpected and well received.

That evening, Osbert and I were eating supper in the dining hall when Sir Ronan entered followed by a man who was most certainly his squire. We made eye contact and Ronan nodded almost imperceptibly to the man behind him, affirming my assumption; I did the same toward Osbert, who was busily sopping up the last of his stew with a piece of bread and took no notice of the exchange.

"That man who just entered . . . ," I nudged Osbert. "I believe that's Sir Ronan Grai?"

Osbert looked up from his food. "Aye, m'lord. 'Twere his squire—right behind him there—what showed me to the captain this morning to get our lodgings." He returned his attention to the last morsels of his meal.

One more part of my secret mission accomplished without requiring any artifice on my part. The next bit felt a little trickier. "I understand Grandfather assigned him here personally. If he or his squire ever asks to see me for any reason, please make sure I see them right away . . . as a courtesy to the king." I paused, then added, "Just as you would for Lord Harold."

"Aye, m'lord," he replied without looking up and with a mouthful of food.

I patted myself on the back for having navigated this bit without drawing too much attention to the request. One thing I knew for sure—Osbert never forgets such things.

I woke with the sunrise to find that Osbert, Edric, and Toly already had the horses saddled and our packs ready. We headed up the middle gully, following a narrow track clearly used by the animals. It wound its way, as streams do, through the valleys, but always moving higher and higher into the hills. Eventually the track began to disappear, so the horses had to pick their way carefully. By mid-afternoon, we reached a barrier, a landslide . . . perhaps more than one . . . having blocked the stream bed with rocks and debris.

While Osbert and the others speculated about how we might get over or around, I dismounted and headed up the hill in the direction from which the debris seemed to have fallen. Did I hear something? I stopped in my tracks and shouted to the others, "Quiet for a moment. Listen." And then I heard it again . . . the sound of running water. Scrambling up the debris pile as quickly as I could, I let out a loud whoop when I reached the top and saw a fast flowing stream on the other side, coming from the west but making a sharp bend here to flow north instead. Harold was right about this having been a source of water for the old lake. The landslides created a barrier, and the stream had to find a new path down the hills.

We camped for the night. In the morning, Toly and Edric took measurements and made drawings and then we headed back down to the camp. It would require Harold's expertise to know if there were a reasonable way to coax the stream back to its ancient route. The sun had set before we got all the way back, but a full moon provided plenty of light for us to follow the track for the last couple of miles.

Excited to share our findings with Harold, I woke just after sunrise, grabbed our drawings and measurements, and headed to my uncle's quarters. His "Come!" in response to my knock sounded gruff and angry. Inside, I found him pacing back and forth, Captain Arnald standing to one side with a rather nasty bruise on his cheek.

Seeing me, Harold stopped abruptly. "Alfred, it's you. I hadn't expected you back so soon."

"Nor I, but we have the good news you were hoping for."

"I'm afraid it will have to wait. I have some rather unpleasant business to attend to this morning. I'm glad you're here, though. You should witness this as well."

I was completely puzzled.

"The whole camp is to assemble outside the dining hall in just a few minutes. I'd like you to be there, standing beside Arnald."

"Of course, Uncle, whatever you wish."

He softened his tone for a moment. "You'll see what's afoot soon enough. Once we get this bad business over with, I really *am* eager to hear what you've found."

Outside the dining hall, workers, knights, and squires were milling around a small platform. Osbert found me there. "There be bad doings while we be gone, sir. Lots of rumors, but I dinna' know what be the truth of the matter."

"I think we're about to find out, Osbert." As Harold and Arnald stepped up onto the platform, I took my place beside them as requested.

"Bring Sir Ronan Grai." Harold's voice was stentorian.

From a tool storage hut nearby, Sir Ronan emerged, hands tied behind his back, guarded by two knights. They brought him to stand facing Harold.

"Sir Ronan, you've been warned twice for insubordination," Harold spoke so there would be no doubt of anyone hearing his every word. "Yesterday, you struck a superior officer. This was witnessed by the two men who are now your guards. Such conduct violates the code of our knights, and I will not condone it under my command."

Ronan stood with his head bowed.

"Sir Ronan Grai, by the authority vested in me by His Grace the king to maintain order and enforce our laws in this endeavor, I hereby strip you of your knighthood. You are henceforth simply Ronan Grai and have none of the privileges or honors associated with a knight of our realm."

Harold paused for effect as a murmur ran through the crowd. "You shall collect your belongings, and you and your squire shall quit these premises before midday. You shall not show your face again at this project. You shall not represent yourself as a knight at any place or to any person in this realm. You shall not receive any knight's retirement honors." At this, all the knights, including the captain, turned their backs on Ronan.

Harold finished. "Send your squire to my quarters for your pay. I don't wish to see your face again." Then he stepped off the platform and beckoned for the captain and me to follow him.

The crowd began to quietly disperse. I could hear the voices of the foremen calling their workers to return to a normal day's activity.

Back in Harold's quarters, I shut the door behind us as Harold crossed to his writing table and fell into a chair. "Thank heaven that's over," he sounded relieved. "I'm sorry, Arnald, that you had to endure that. Father warned me he might be trouble, but I never suspected it would go beyond verbal insubordination."

"You're not to blame, my lord. And I thank you for acting as you have to preserve discipline."

"It's a shame, really," mused Harold. "He's an exceptional engineer. His solution for the sluice gates was inspired. And his career until lately has been exemplary. I wonder what it is that makes a good man go over the edge like that." A knock at the door interrupted his musings. "No doubt that's Ronan's squire come for his pay. I really don't want to see him. Alfred, answer the door if you will and give him this purse." He tossed me a small leather pouch that contained a few coins.

I opened the door to find the squire, accompanied by one of the knights who had been guarding Ronan. "From Lord Harold," I said, handing him the purse and closing the door immediately to return to my uncle and the captain.

Harold sat more upright and placed his hands on the table in front of him, visibly shaking off the unpleasantness of the preceding events.

"So Alfred, show me what you've found. I could use some good news."

Arnald moved as if to leave, but Harold detained him. "Stay, Arnald, if you will. Depending on what Alfred has to show us, we may need to make some new plans."

We sat around the table, where I spread out Edric's map and landscape drawings and the notes of our measurements. "The stream was full and flowing rapidly," I told them, "so it's not that the source of water has dried up . . . it's just changed direction."

"This is perfect! I didn't know you could draw, Alfred."

"I can't, uncle. At least not like this. Edric gets the credit for all your drawings."

"Good measurements, too. It will help us form some preliminary notion of what we're dealing with before we go up there. You're not an engineer. How did you know to measure both sides of the debris pile?"

"I can't take the credit there, either. That was Toly. In fact, I think the overall credit goes to Captain Arnald here for knowing what kind of skills I might need if we found something interesting and assigning the right squires to go with us."

Harold laughed out loud. "That's why I keep him around, right, Arnald?" The captain just smiled.

"So you've actually seen the site, Alfred. What do you think?"

"Well, as you said, I'm no engineer. So all I have are possibilities. I don't know what's actually doable."

"Then let's hear the possibilities."

"Well, I think maybe if the debris could be breached, the stream might be quite happy to resume its old flow eastward toward the reservoir. There seems to be some sort of ridge under the rubble that may have kept the stream flowing this way in times past. But it has definitely cut something of a channel on its northbound route, so it might be necessary to block off that route to re-establish the old path. I don't know if the cleared rubble could be used for that.

"Then there's the question of how to prevent future landslides from just recreating the problem all over again. It all seems like an awful lot of work."

"It will be worth it, though, if it's in any way feasible," said Harold. "My intuition says that stream is fed by snow melt from high in the peaks. If we can get it to empty into our new lake, then we can keep the reservoir full even in the years when we don't have good rain.

"Just to be thorough, though, Alfred, you and Osbert check out that other gully. Don't go any farther with just the two of you than half a day's ride. I'm guessing you won't even have to go that far if the southern gully is any indication.

"Arnald, get some rough measurements of the width of that debris pile from what we have here and then take a crew up to assess things on site. Let's see what it would take to execute Alfred's 'possibilities.'"

Life in the project camp settled into a familiar routine. Our exploration of the northern gully proved Harold's suspicions correct, so all the attention turned to removing the landslide debris and rerouting the stream. Some of the work could begin straightaway, but the final release of the stream to flow into the lake would have to wait until all the mortar in the dam structure was fully cured and the supporting banks of earth on the north and south ends were finished. If Harold was right about the stream being fed by snow-melt, then the flow should be reduced or stopped by late winter, and it would be easier to change its course.

Harold also showed me the work that had begun on the canals. Both were being built simultaneously so as not to favor any one group of farmers and landholders. It's a slow process, so only about five miles of each canal was complete. It would go faster once the dam was finished and workers could be diverted to the canals. Some farmers, it seemed, were already starting to build their trenches. I discovered at least two problems, which I described in a letter to my grandfather.

Sir,

I believe your concerns about the reservoir project to be well-founded. The concept, as you say, seems sound enough, the engineering is superb, and the execution proceeds at a rapid pace. The risk appears to be in the realm of human nature and the fears men have, of which we have so often spoken.

The first problem I see is that not all farmers and landholders have direct access to the canals. Those at greater distance from a canal will be beholden to their neighbors to pass water through.

The second problem involves the behavior of water as well as the behavior of men. Water flows inexorably to the lowest place it can find. So if some dig their trenches deeper than others or if trenches are dug significantly deeper than the level of the bottom of the canals, more water will flow to whatever is deepest, depriving others of their fair share. In years of significant drought, this could even result in there being no water at all in the more easterly portions of the canals.

It seems to me that some rules will be needed for how everything is to be done. And perhaps some inducement to obey the rules.

Respectfully,

Alfred

I re-read my letter twice then folded the paper, poured hot wax, and applied my seal. Osbert would make sure it was in the message pouch for the courier scheduled to leave the next day. A letter to Gwen was already in that pouch.

Osbert enthusiastically embraced the squires' scheme of shared duties. Shortly after we returned from our gully exploration, he and Toly went to market day in the nearest town and returned full of news and gossip about Ronan Grai's dismissal. Ronan and his squire had gone from here to the town, bought supplies, and departed immediately on the road toward the Peaks. Rumors about their plans were rampant. Some said he intended to offer his services to the King of Peaks; others said he meant to join up with Ranulf and his sons. Some said he had a wife and family in the Peaks; others said he simply wanted to go somewhere he could lead a simple life, untroubled by his past. Likely, we'd never know the truth of the matter.

Yet that called into question the completion of my secret mission for my grandfather. I was tempted to write to him that Sir Ronan's conduct had put an end to any hopes he may have had of receiving a message. Then I remembered his caution: "The circumstances may not be what you expect." So I decided to give things more time and see what might develop.

Eight days later, the courier returned with messages from the castle. Of my two, I chose to read the one from my grandfather first.

My dear Alfred,

I write this in haste so that it may come back to you with this courier. Your evaluation affirms my concerns. Speak with Harold and get his specifications for the rules that will be needed. I trust to your usual instincts for tact and diplomacy for this conversation. Advise me as soon as we have the necessary details, and I'll move forward with the Council.

My other letter was from Gwen and I made my way to our hut to savor it in complete privacy.

My dearest darling Alfred,

I miss you incredibly but know you must do your duty. So since you can't be here, some news from home.

Your parents are well and send their love. Your mates are as ever, but I think they'll be glad of your return. Phillip insisted I should tell you that you must get on with whatever you're doing and hurry home else he risks bankrupting himself paying for what should be your rounds of drinks at the tavern.

Your cousin Avelina has been at court since shortly after you left, and we are becoming quite good friends. It's widely expected that she and Richard are to be betrothed at Christmas time. Yet another good reason for you to come home.

All is well at the kennel. Brother Adam wants to use more of the new blood lines, so I've brought Morgana to live with us. She's a constant companion to me and a delightful reminder of you.

And now for the most wonderful news of all. It's definite. There's a child on the way. I am so very happy, Alfred, and I trust you are, too. It will be born in the early spring, so I encourage you to finish your work there and hurry home to me in time for the birth. I've told your parents and grandfather as well as my family. It's certain enough now that you may tell anyone you wish.

In a month or two, we should start considering what to name our little one. This should give you something to think about in the evenings when I'm not there to distract you in other ways.

I miss you terribly. I miss our walks in the woods. I miss our cozy suppers together. I miss our evenings in front of the fire. Most especially I miss your presence in our bed and all the delightful things we do there. I miss seeing your face when I wake in the morning. I miss snuggling next to you as I fall asleep at night.

I love you more than anything in this world and pray that God will look after you and keep you safe and bring you back to me soonest.

All my love, your
Gwen

I read her letter again and again. It was true. I was going to be a father. I had thought I'd want to shout this from the rooftops as soon as I knew; but I found that, in these surroundings, I wanted to keep the news to myself as something private and precious for now. Soon enough, no doubt, I'd do that shouting. But in that moment, all I wanted to do was to write a deeply loving reply to her that would go in the next pouch.

The next day, I spoke with Harold about the need for rules to guide use of the water from the reservoir. He wholeheartedly agreed. "This is the sort of thing at which you and your father are much better than I am. You know, I used to envy Edward that skill; but lately I've come to realize that a king doesn't have to have all the skills himself. He just has to be astute enough to recognize and admit his weaknesses and to know who has those abilities and is reliable to use them for the right ends."

I recall being surprised—both that my uncle had this level of self-awareness and that he'd shared it so openly with me.

"So, Alfred," he continued, "I hope I can count on you when the time comes to provide advice and counsel to an imperfect monarch?"

"I'll always be happy to be at your service, Uncle."

By now, more than a month had passed since Osbert and I first arrived. Harold gave me responsibility for making the camp ready for winter, which meant finishing the little stone building that houses the kitchens, completing a proper shelter for the horses with a loft to store the hay and fodder out of reach of any animal that might wander down from the hills, and constructing another stone hut for storing our winter food out of the easy reach of vermin.

Once the dam and buildings were complete, the masons and stone cutters would return home and not winter over at the camp. The huts that had served as lodgings for the senior craftsmen would be converted to barracks. There'd be eight or ten men to a hut, but even that slight crowding would be preferable to winter quarters in a tent. The carpenters fitted shutters that could be closed against the chill winds and snow.

Yesterday we saw a horseman on the ridge above the southern gully. He was just sitting there, apparently watching the activity. It was the first time I'd seen such a thing since I arrived. Captain Arnald said it was the first time he'd seen such a thing since the work here began, but he didn't seem overly concerned or alarmed. Two days later a horseman appeared on a hillside above the northern gully. The captain's attitude changed to one of concern.

For the next three days, there were no further appearances of our mysterious horsemen and tensions began to relax. But today, four days after the last sighting, two horsemen appeared at the top of a hill near the dry streambed, in a place that would lie between us and the work crew at the site of the landslides. Arnald was now alarmed and asked me to join him in Harold's quarters.

"Who could they be?" asked Harold.

"I don't know, my lord, but I don't like it. There's no way to know where they've come from or even how many there are. Is it just two? Or do the sightings we've had mean there are four? Or are there more? One thing seems certain . . . they're clearly observing us for some reason."

"I don't want to create an atmosphere of fear here until we have a better idea of what they're up to," said Harold. "What do you recommend, Arnald?"

"Let me take a patrol up into the hills. Half the troop and a couple of squires should be sufficient. That should be enough to chase away or capture a small gang or to defend ourselves if we run into trouble.

The rest can stay here under your command. Before we leave, I'll make arrangements for the watch and put my men on alert for anything out of the ordinary."

"How soon can you be ready?"

"We can depart by midday tomorrow. I think the sooner we resolve this business the better."

"I quite agree. Get to it then. Even if you wind up chasing them away, try to discover where they're from and what they're up to. Godspeed, Arnald. You and your men come back safely."

Back in our hut—which Osbert and I would occupy alone while the captain was gone—I made sure that my bow and a sack of arrows were placed where they'd be in easy reach. When we returned to the hut after supper, Osbert clearly noticed my arrangements but said nothing.

Three days passed after the patrol's departure—three days in which we saw no more horsemen. It was tempting to hope that the mere presence of Arnald's men had been enough to send them on their way. As the supply patrol was scheduled to arrive in ten days' time, we doubled the effort to complete the work on the camp buildings—tiring work that left everyone exhausted at day's end and drove us to seek our beds very soon after supper.

It was the new moon and I expected to sleep especially well in the dark night. Sometime in the middle of the night, I was awakened by Osbert shaking my shoulder. Even in the darkness, I could see him holding a finger to his lips to ensure that I made no undue noise.

"What is it?" I whispered.

"Ye've a visitor, m'lord. Ye be telling me once that if Ronan Grai or his squire ever be wanting to see ye, I were to make it happen right away." He paused. "The squire be here right now, m'lord. With an urgent message, he be saying."

I sat up on the edge of my cot. "Bring him in, Osbert, and leave us to talk."

"I not be liking to leave ye, m'lord; we dinna' know what he be here fer."

"It will be alright, Osbert. Just wait outside where I can call you to come quickly if I need you."

"Very well, m'lord." He moved silently to the door, which he'd left ajar, and beckoned to the man outside to enter. Then he left and closed the door quietly behind him.

Still speaking no louder than a whisper, I greeted the visitor. "You wish to speak to me?"

"Aye, m'lord," he replied. "I have a message fer ye from Sir Ronan." I noted the use of the honorific, but saw no need to correct it. "He says ye'll know what to do with the information."

"What's the message?"

"They'll attack Sunday morning, just as the camp is awakening, before men have time to get their boots on and gather their wits about them. There'll be twelve. Ranulf and his sons, six more who've joined the gang, and of course Sir Ronan and I have to stay with them."

"Is there anything more you can tell me?"

"That be the whole of the message, m'lord. And now I best be getting back. Sir Ronan has the last watch, and I can sneak back while he's on duty with no one being the wiser that I was gone."

I now realized there was much more to Ronan Grai's dismissal than simple insubordination. But I didn't have time to think about what. This was the mission Grandfather had sent me here for, and I had to act right away.

"Thank you, squire. Tell Sir Ronan," I used the honorific intentionally knowing that this man would convey my message exactly and wanting Ronan to know that I understood a lot must be at stake, "that I'll convey his message to the king urgently. Now be off and keep yourself and your master safe."

The door opened and the squire disappeared into the darkness as Osbert returned. "M'lord?"

"I have some work to do, Osbert. Fetch me a candle and then wait outside to be sure no one comes in. If you can close the shutters quietly so the guard doesn't see the candlelight, please do that right away. As soon as I'm finished, I'll tell you everything because then I'll have a task for you."

While Osbert closed the shutters, I took pen and paper from my pack. On the first sheet, I wrote the letters of the alphabet in four rows, leaving space between the rows. Then, under each letter, I wrote the letter that comes three letters later in the alphabet.

A B C D E F G H
d e f g h i j k

I J K L M N O P
l m n o p q r s

Q R S T U V W
t u v w x y z

X Y Z
a b c

Grandfather taught me about the great Julius Caesar's code for sending secret messages. He'd recognize the code and know that Caesar always used the offset of three. It wouldn't take him long to prepare a key like mine and decode the message.

And so I began to write.

Vxqgdb qhaw. Dwwdfh hduob pruqlqj dv phq dzdnh. Wzhoyh phq lq jdqj. Udqxoi, vrqv, vlu qhz lq jdqj, Urqdq dqg vtxluh. Doiuhg

I folded the paper and sealed it with wax but didn't affix my seal. Grandfather would receive it directly from Osbert's hand and could be certain it came from me. I doused the candle and helped Osbert open the shutters; then we retreated back inside the hut.

We continued to whisper, in case anyone should pass by outside. "I have a mission for you Osbert. I can't tell you all the details because I don't know them all myself. But I'll tell you everything I can and rely on your discretion.

"Ronan Grai's squire brought information that must get to the king urgently but in complete secrecy. I've prepared the message . . . it's there on the table. I want you to put it inside your stocking, before you put on your boots. That way if anyone should waylay you and remove your boots, they won't easily become aware that you have a message secreted on your person.

"In the morning, you'll collect the message pouch and ride out on what will appear to everyone as a routine courier trip. I'll take care of the explanations as to why a courier run is needed right away.

"Ride normally as you leave the camp and so long as you think you might be in sight of anyone observing from the hills above us. When you go through the towns, ride as you would on a normal courier run. But between the towns, ride like the wind.

"We need to get this message to my grandfather in three days' time . . . less, if possible. Do your best, but don't exhaust your horse – you need him to get you there. I'll give you a purse. If your horse gets too tired, stable him with a blacksmith and buy a fresh one. You can collect yours on your return journey. Do whatever you must to get to the castle as quickly as a man can.

"When you arrive, give this message to no one but the king. Not my father, not the king's squire nor his guard, not even the Lady Gwendolyn. Only the king."

"What if I not be able to see the king right away?" Osbert asked.

"I assure you, Osbert, the king will see you immediately, no matter what time of day or night you arrive. I don't know why, but I think he expects this message and will have told his guards and his squire to admit you as soon as you arrive."

"Do I wait for an answer, m'lord?"

"I don't know, Osbert. The king will tell you what to do next. I don't know why, but I think this is something of great import to the kingdom. I *do* know that there's no one I can rely on more to complete this mission."

"Why ye not be taking the message yerself, m'lord? That way ye not be needing to write it down."

"That's true, Osbert. But if I leave the camp, everyone will notice and all kinds of rumors will spread. If you leave on a courier run, no one will think twice about it."

"There be truth in that fer certain, m'lord. Ye can count on me. Now, let's be sleeping fer what be left of the night. I be thinking I not be sleeping much fer the next two days."

Somehow Osbert did manage to sleep. I, on the other hand, lay awake, my mind racing. The business with Sir Ronan, Ranulf's gang, Ronan and his squire turning up with the gang . . . something was afoot that I couldn't quite piece together. And I also remembered my grandfather's other admonition: "You are to take no other action on your own initiative." That was clearly going to be the hardest part of his guidance to follow.

Saturday evening. Since I sent Osbert on his way, we'd seen no more of the horsemen in the hills. But neither had Captain Arnald's patrol returned. We knew not if the horsemen had satisfied their curiosity, if the patrol had driven them away, if they'd been captured, or if something untoward had happened to our comrades.

I alone knew that something dreadful might befall us on the morrow if my grandfather hadn't been able to act to prevent it. I reminded myself constantly of his admonition.

Supper finished, I found myself walking alone back toward my hut. Seeing Harold just ahead in the company of his squire, I quickened my pace, calling out, "Uncle!"

He paused and turned in my direction. Catching up to them I said, "I'm really not ready to retire or return to my hut alone. What say you to some company and conversation?"

"I . . . "

He seemed to hesitate so I finished his sentence for him, " . . . have no pressing work that won't keep until tomorrow. And *I* have in my hut a bottle of fine wine from Grandfather's cellar that I talked the steward into giving me should there be something to celebrate here. With the dam complete for all practical purposes, the ancient water source solved, your laws in progress . . . "

He held up a hand to interrupt me. "Correction . . . *your* laws."

"*Our* laws, then," I continued, "and the winterization of the camp almost complete, it seems there is indeed something to celebrate." I paused. "And I can think of no one I'd rather share this bottle with."

He didn't answer immediately, seeming to weigh his overall responsibilities and the prospect of fine wine in the balance. "Alfred, you do know how to tempt a man. It's been months since I've had anything the likes of what comes from Father's cellar. And you've made a good case that some small celebration is in order."

Turning to his squire, he said, "Milo, I'll be with Lord Alfred if I'm needed. Off with you and enjoy an evening to yourself."

Inside the hut, I retrieved my pack from under my cot, removed the bottle of wine, and found a couple of cups. "It's not Gwen's fine glassware," I remarked, "but I suspect the wine will be no less tasty."

Harold looked around the room while I poured and took note of my weapon at the ready. "Preparing for an attack?" he asked.

"Not particularly," I replied, handing him a cup of wine. "I've just been a little uneasy what with the mysterious horsemen and staying alone in this hut with everyone away. Couldn't help but remember what Cedric drummed into our heads: 'Remember lads, you'll regret not being prepared for something far longer than you'll regret preparations that turn out to be for naught.'"

Harold roared with laughter and plopped himself down on the cot across from me. "Oh, my God, lad, how many times did I hear that myself! I wonder how many scores of knights have had that dogma burned into their consciousness?" He raised his cup. "To Cedric and preparations."

I followed suit. "To Cedric."

"Oh, that is exceedingly good," he avowed after tasting the wine. "I've been up here so long I'd almost forgotten how excellent Father's cellar really is."

"Quite appropriate to the occasion, I should say. Now I'd like to propose a toast." I raised my cup. "To what you've accomplished here. It's a remarkable solution to what could have become a terrible problem down the road in the absence of preparations."

He raised his cup to mine. "Thank you, Alfred. I have to admit some pride in what we've achieved here."

"Deservedly so." And we drank to Harold's success.

We sat in silence for a few minutes, savoring the wine. I topped up our cups.

"So what will you do once the project is complete in the spring?" I asked.

"Don't know," he replied. "There's no doubt I'll need to come here from time to time to check on things. And there'll be supervision needed for the completion of the canals. I'm sure your grandfather will have some new assignment up his sleeve . . . he always does." He paused for a moment, then chuckled. "Knowing him, I suspect my next assignment is going to be to find a wife."

"Without prying, I must say there are many who wonder why you've never remarried."

"I take no offense. You're only saying aloud, Alfred, what everyone wonders in private. What I, myself, sometimes wonder." He drank from his cup and looked at the ceiling pensively.

"You know, at first, my excuse was that I should wait until I'm king and then make a politically advantageous marriage. Of course, since it looks like Father is going to be the second Methuselah . . . " We both chuckled.

"Don't mistake me. His longevity and continuing vitality please me greatly. It's just that I'm now almost twice the age at which he ascended the throne, so that excuse is no longer plausible. I know that people look to me to produce an heir, ensuring the succession. But it wouldn't be a bad thing for the kingdom if Edward were to succeed. He would make an excellent king."

"I've no doubt he would, but that would make John next in line. And there are many in the kingdom — my father included, I daresay — who would be exceptionally grateful to you for taking steps to avert that disaster."

"Put that way, how can I argue with you?" Another thoughtful pause. "In truth, Alfred . . . and I've never shared this confidence with anyone before . . . I'm extraordinarily uncomfortable in the society of women. I know not how to converse with them. I have no interest in hours of prattling about fashion or the latest gossip of the court or the running of a household. And they seem to have no interest or ability to understand the things that I find interesting, fascinating, or mentally challenging.

"I'm not a romantic. I have no interest in reading love poems. I'm not a brutish lover, but I know not the language of love and romance." He was quiet for a long time, and I respected his silence there in the dark.

"My Berengaria was extraordinary—perhaps one of a kind. She was from my mother's native land, you know—the Kingdom Across the Southern Sea. I believe my mother may even have had a strong hand in choosing her for me.

"She could draw me out to talk of all the things that interested me; and she could listen for hours on end. She was kind and gentle. In the marriage bed, she was willing, if not passionate. I know our partnership was one-sided—that I drew more from it than I was able to give to her. But she was always cheerful, always happy, always there for me." He was quiet again for some moments.

"When she died, my heart was brutally torn asunder. I never realized until then how very deeply I loved her. And then it was too late to tell her. I don't know if I could endure such pain again."

We both sat quietly in the dark. I understood that he was sharing with me the deepest secrets of his soul.

At length I ventured quietly, "Perhaps now that there are more educated women you might be more successful in finding the right kind of partner—someone more your equal whom you could love in a different way." I let this thought take shape in his mind for some minutes before I spoke again. "Consider my Gwen. She's educated, well read, able to converse on so many topics, none of which involve frocks or frivolities." He chuckled softly. "Perhaps when we're back home . . . perhaps you might spend some time with us . . . see the kind of marriage we have."

"I'd like that very much, Alfred. I've heard only the very best of your lady and would like to know her better.

"You know," he added, "your grandfather does everything with a definite purpose in mind—often more than one. It occurs to me that perhaps his secondary purpose in sending you here was to give us an opportunity to know each other better."

"Then that's my good fortune," I replied. After the intimacy of his revelations, it saddened me that I couldn't tell him that Grandfather had yet a third purpose in sending me here.

It was getting late, and we'd emptied the bottle of wine. "Stay here tonight," I said. "I'd be glad of the company."

I worried he might decline, but he made no attempt to leave. "Ah, well, Milo knows where to find me. As tired as I am, you needn't ask twice."

We lay on our cots, boots still on, pulled up the blankets, and were soon sound asleep.

It was the time of year when the sun rose noticeably later each day. I awakened with the sun and with an overwhelming sense of foreboding. I lay in my cot and listened. The camp was quiet save for the chirping of the birds. Normal for a Sunday, but I still couldn't shake the feeling that something was very wrong. Harold was still asleep.

I slipped quietly out of bed and looked out the window on my side of the hut. Nothing seemed unusual or out of place. Then I looked out the other window and my heart started pounding. There were three men creeping toward Harold's hut, looking around furtively as if to see if they'd been detected—men I'd never seen before.

I touched Harold's shoulder to wake him and like a good soldier, he was instantly alert. Seeing my finger pressed to my lips, he didn't speak . . . just looked at me questioningly.

"Something's up," I whispered. "There are strangers in the camp, and I think they're looking for you." I pointed to the window and he sneaked a quick look.

"Stay here, stay quiet, and keep your head down," I told him, grabbing my bow and sack of arrows and exiting through the window on the opposite side. As I peered carefully around the corner of the hut, I saw that the intruders had arrived at Harold's quarters, and one of them was peering into the window. They must have sneaked past the sentries or—and my heart chilled at this prospect—captured or killed them.

Could I get off three shots quickly enough and accurately enough to disable them all? I'm a good marksman, but had never had reason to practice the speed that's the hallmark of our best bowmen.

Before I could decide, the intruders realized no one was in the hut and let out what I can only describe as a shrill war cry. From the distance came men on horseback, riding at speed toward the camp and screaming the same war cry. I could only surmise that the plan was for kidnap and, if that failed, all-out attack.

The screaming awakened the camp, and I saw knights emerge in the front doors of two separate huts. Each was immediately felled, one with an arrow in the shoulder and one in the leg. The horsemen had brought mounts for the original three, and now they were all criss-crossing the camp.

I saw two men headed for the paddock, presumably to release our horses. Somehow, even from the back, I recognized Ronan Grai and his squire. Confident that Ronan would find some way to delay what he'd been ordered to do, I turned my attention back to the mayhem all around.

I heard the sound of knights yelling at each other as they armed themselves and prepared to engage. To my left, I saw Harold, who seemed to have ignored my advice, running from the door of his hut, armed and shouting orders as he took command.

The intruders rode back and forth, slashing their swords at anything in their path. They slashed the tents that were the laborers' lodgings, sending men screaming in all directions for safety. The craftsmen mostly hunkered down inside their huts, but a few craftsmen and laborers grabbed tools or threw rocks, trying to fend off the attackers. It was hard to get a clear shot at the intruders for fear of hitting one of our own people.

As I was looking for an opportunity to shoot, I noticed a group of riders appear high in the hills. I sensed, even without careful observation, that this was Captain Arnald's patrol on their way to help. But from where they were, it would be at least half an hour before they arrived, so we had to fend for ourselves.

Over the din, I heard Harold shouting, "Alfred! The horses!"

Instantly, I knew he wasn't referring to our own horses. If I could take out the mounts of the intruders, then they'd have to fight on foot, removing their advantage over our knights.

My first two shots went wildly astray as I tried to compensate for the direction of motion and the speed of the riders. Thankfully, there was no wind to further complicate things. My third shot found its mark squarely in the chest of a horse that was just turning in my direction. The fourth took a horse in the shoulder and he went down, dumping his rider on the ground. I'd finally found the right amount to lead the riders in order to hit my targets.

As I took out another horse, I noticed an intruder on foot with a vicious looking knife in his hand moving toward Harold, whose back was turned to his pursuer. He seemed to be an older man, with long grey hair, but he also seemed wiry and extremely fit. I notched an arrow and aimed, ready to fire should he threaten my uncle. He quickened his pace, and I loosed my arrow.

All was suddenly in slow motion. It seemed the attacker was gaining on Harold faster than my arrow was gaining on its target. But just as the man raised his knife hand and started to run, the arrow found its mark, squarely in his back. I knew it had pierced his heart; but before he fell, he looked back in the direction from which death came to him, and I got a good look at his face. He was about the age of my grandfather, and he had a livid scar on his left cheek. Surely this must have been Ranulf.

Harold looked around and realized his lucky escape. I shouted to him, "Ronan Grai! Friend, not foe!" and could only hope he heard me above the din of the fight.

As I turned my attention toward the remaining horsemen, I heard a thunderous pounding of hooves coming from the direction of the main track. Were there to be more of them? As I notched an arrow to resume taking out our attacker's horses, I glanced in that direction and realized that the noise was a large troop of knights riding hard and carrying the king's banner.

That was the last thing I saw before I was hit on the head from behind and my world slowly went black.

When I came to my senses as a captive, I was confident of finding a way to catch my captor off guard and either overpower him or use my speed and stamina to run away. What I hadn't bargained on was his fixation on a ransom. Now, all these many weeks later, with my prospects dwindling by the day, I can only hope I'm wrong about my grandfather's resolve. Ransom, it seems, is my only chance. But there is no way for him to know that.

Yet another full moon has passed, marking my third month in captivity. It also means that the solstice has passed and the new year has arrived. Just after midday on the day following the new moon, I hear the key turn in the lock. The door is opened and Ralf bursts in looking hale and quite happy. I wonder if perhaps he's received his ransom after all.

"Well, well," he says. "You're still here. Rather thought you might be." And he chuckles at his own little joke.

Then he wrinkles his nose and looks me up and down. "My God, you stink!" he exclaims. It's been months since I've had a bath, and I've been living with my own stench for so long that I no longer notice it.

"Guard!" he shouts at the top of his lungs.

I hear running in the corridor and fumbling with the key in the lock. The guard must think this is a cry of alarm. When the door opens, Ralf points to me and says, "Take him out and clean him up. He stinks to high heaven."

As the guard starts to lead me out, he adds, "Mind you, don't get any water in his boots. I don't need his feet to rot off. And don't leave him freezing in wet clothes. I don't need him dead either."

I'm taken down to the kitchens, where a second guard is waiting, and out a side door where there's a water trough. The prospect of being doused in that cold water has me shivering already. One of the guards yanks my leg shackles high up my boots, to where the thickness of my calf inhibits any further movement. Then he tugs hard again. I fear my feet will go numb, but at least this should prevent my boots filling with water.

One guard takes me under the arms, the other grabs my ankles, and they lower me into the trough, taking care to keep my boots out of the water. The water is icy, and I gasp involuntarily. The guard at my head mimes holding one's breath then pushes my head under the water and scrubs at my hair and beard. He releases me and I come up blubbering, but I can breathe while he scrubs my clothes, arms, and torso with a rough brush. Then they lift me out of the trough and hold me above it while water drips from my clothes and hair. My teeth are chattering and I'm visibly shaking from the cold.

They take me into the kitchen, where it's blissfully warm, and seat me in a chair in front of the fire. One of the kitchen maids is summoned to bring a towel to take more of the water from my hair and beard. The cook hands me a cup full of hot broth, which I drink gratefully with shaking hands. Slowly, the warmth of the fire and the broth diminish my shaking and shivering.

The extra guard leaves, and the other one sits at the work table and flirts with the kitchen maids. When I've stopped shaking, I stand and turn my back to the fire to let that side of my clothes dry and to better dry my hair. My feet are, indeed, going slightly numb with the tightness of the shackles, so as soon as my trousers are reasonably dry, I shove the shackles back down around my ankles where they're looser. The feeling quickly returns to my feet.

It takes more than an hour, but when the guard finally decides that I'm dry and he won't incur Ralf's displeasure, I'm taken back to my cell. Ralf is there. He sticks his nose in the air and sniffs. "That's better." Then he looks me up and down. "But he still looks terrible. Get someone up here to cut that hair and beard some. Nothing fancy . . . just so he looks like he's not been tortured." Once again I wonder if he has, in fact, received the ransom.

The guard returns with some kind of shears and whacks at my hair and beard. I can tell by what falls on the floor that it's ragged, but at least it's shorter.

Ralf appraises me once again. "Hmph," he grunts. "That'll have to do." He marches out the door, followed by the guard, and the key turns in the lock.

Despite the ordeal, being somewhat cleaner is welcome. I wrap myself in my blankets to keep out the chill and settle in once again to my daily routine.

The moon is just past its first quarter before I see Ralf again. He arrives with the scullery maid, carrying a rope, and seems to be in a dour mood. I can guess what's coming.

He starts to tie the rope into the loop on my collar. "Your ransom hasn't come," he says, fixing his knots, "and Owen's patched up his quarrel with his neighbor, so it's time we move on."

He tosses one of the blankets at me and I catch it awkwardly. "You can use that for a cloak."

He leads me out, down the stairs, and to the stables where his horse is already saddled and waiting. Owen is there to see us off. "No need for you to go," he says. "You're welcome here as long as you'd like."

"Thanks, but no," replies Ralf, mounting his horse. "I said I'd keep taking him farther and farther from home, and I'm a man of my word."

"That you are, Ralf," says Owen. "Godspeed. I hope you do get your fortune. Come back here any time you want."

As we set off into the winter cold, I decide there's no harm in asking again. "Who are you, Ralf? And why are you doing this to me?"

"Perhaps it's time you should know," he replies. "I'm the third son of Sir Ranulf, once a knight of your kingdom. My father," he pauses for a long moment, "is dead, killed by your arrow during the raid on the camp in the foothills." So it was, indeed, Ranulf from whom I saved Harold. And now the look of recognition makes sense. It wasn't for me but for the man coming up behind me, preparing to take his revenge.

"You," he points a finger directly at me, "are Alfred, son of Lord Edward. All your attempts to deny it won't change that fact. You took my father from me. I've taken you from your father. And from all the rest of your family. They must pay if they want you back." And with this, his volubility comes to an abrupt end. While it changes nothing, I find some satisfaction in finally knowing why I'm a captive.

We return to the main road by the same track that brought us here and resume our wanderings ever west. Day after day after day. I think by now we must be nearing the end of the earth. Presumably looking out for his own welfare more than mine, Ralf manages to find us some sort of shelter most nights—a broken down shack with walls enough to protect us from the wind . . . occasionally a nice warm barn . . . sometimes a horse shelter or makeshift stable. But every morning, we resume our trek westward.

The moon is approaching its last quarter. Tonight we find a stable for shelter. There are no animals here, but there's plenty of hay for Ralf's horse and for making warm beds. I'm given my supper of bread and water and chained to one of the support posts for the night.

The next morning I waken slowly to the sunlight coming in through the small windows high in the rafters. Something is wrong. Normally, I'm kicked awake at dawn.

I open my eyes slowly, anxious as to what I might see. Looking around, I see . . . nothing. No sign of Ralf or his horse. No sign of his pack. No sign that he was ever here. Yet I'm still chained to the post. I struggle to my feet and look around again. On top of a barrel in the corner of the stable is half a loaf of bread and a small wedge of cheese—enough to give me hope, but no way to get to it.

Anger and panic rising simultaneously, I use the chain between my hands to pull violently at the post, trying to free myself. The noise from above draws my attention to the roof, which is shaking and wobbling and looks as if it might all come down on top of me. No good can come of pulling the roof down on my head. Nor can I expect hope for rescue by someone bringing animals to shelter here. There's no sign anyone's been here recently but us . . . no horse manure, no sheep droppings, no reins or halters or saddles. It could be days or even weeks before someone wanders by. Far too late for me.

Think, Alfred. There must be *some* way to get yourself free. What's within reach? Nothing but hay. I try futilely to pull a hand through its shackle. Maybe if I push against the metal with my boot, the strength in my legs could force it off. All I succeed in doing is jamming the shackle around the top of my hand, which hurts like hell, so I spend the next few minutes gently sliding the metal back over my wrist, which also hurts like hell because the sores have returned since I've been without the kitchen maid's salve.

And then I spot something. There's a loose board at the top of the stall gate nearest me. If I could pull it off, maybe I could use it to reach something farther away. The angle is awkward and my meager rations mean I don't have the strength I once had, but eventually I manage to pry it off. Two of the nails come with it.

Now that I have it, I assess my surroundings again. But there's still nothing within reach, even with the board as a tool, that's of any use.

Think, Alfred! Too bad Ralf didn't see fit to leave you the key.

The nails. I spend what seems like ages prying and pushing and pulling and trying to get the board to split, desperately trying to get the nails out of its clutches. At last I have them. One is bent at almost a right angle, so I toss it aside and start to work with the one that's more or less straight, poking around in the lock, trying to spring something loose. It's not easy because I have to work with my left hand – it's the shackle on my right wrist that has the hinge and lock. After another age, I've gotten nowhere. In all my reading, why didn't I read something about how a lock works? But I can't give up, so I go back to poking and prodding until my hand cramps painfully from holding the nail so tightly.

Think, Alfred! How does a key work? What does it look like?

A shaft with a loop at one end to hang it over a hook or on a ring and something protruding from the side at the opposite end. The bent nail! Where did it land? A bit of rummaging around in the hay and there it is. It takes a few tries, but eventually I feel the nail push against something. I push again and hear a click as the lock falls open. I've done it! I'm free!

And now I can contemplate my situation more rationally. It seems Ralf has indeed abandoned me here, else he would have returned before now. Thinking about his increasingly somber mood over the past few days, I try to work out why. Perhaps he just grew tired of the game. Perhaps I simply became too much trouble. More likely, though, he achieved at least something of his ends. He knows now there'll be no ransom. But he's brought me so far away and I'm in such a weakened state that he's sure I'll never return home. So if he can't have his ransom, at least he will have his revenge.

What he hasn't bargained on is my determination and my knowledge that there will be a child who needs a father. I have no choice but to return.

I put the bread inside my shirt and the cheese in a pocket of my trousers. Looking around for anything else that could provide sustenance, I open the lid of the barrel and find it half-full of oats for the horses that must occasionally be sheltered here. I stuff my pockets as full of oats as I possibly can. Seeing nothing more I can use, I wrap my blanket around me, step out into the wintry day, follow the path down to the road, and turn to the east. My long walk home has begun.

Even with the shackles still on my ankles, walking is much easier now that one hand is free. I haven't gone far when I spy a low stone wall at the edge of a field not far off the road. Surely there'll be a loose stone somewhere that I can use as a hammer. Walking would be even easier if my left wrist wasn't still chained to my ankle. So I set off to investigate.

Finding a loose stone is easy . . . the wall is in poor repair. Doing anything useful with it proves far more difficult. I pound and pound and accomplish nothing more than to chip the stone and tire myself. Whoever forged this chain was a master of his craft. Realizing this is taking precious energy — energy I'll need if I'm to make it home — I abandon the effort and return to the road.

The first night, I eat the cheese. I manage to make the bread last for two more days. Now I have nothing left but the oats. Not wanting them to swell in my stomach and make me ill, I eat one handful in the morning, one at midday, and one at sundown. At the end of three days, the oats are gone. Now I've no choice but to forage where and how I can.

Sometimes there are oak trees near the road with acorns still around that the animals haven't scavenged for winter food. They're easy enough to crack open, but some taste quite bitter. I eat them anyway. If they can sustain the deer, then they surely can help me keep going. Whenever I see a fast flowing stream, I stop to drink from it. There's no way of knowing how far away the next stream might be.

Though the winter days are still short, they're growing perceptibly longer. Despite that, if I find suitable shelter in the afternoon, I stop there for the night. It's the time of year when a storm can blow up unexpectedly, and it would be deadly to be caught out in the open in one of those.

♦ ♦ ♦ ♦ ♦

Today I arrive again at the road that leads to Owen's fortress. Perhaps I can convince one of the fishing boat masters to give me passage, at least as far as the cove below Ernle Manor. That would certainly be the fastest way home. As I turn down the road, the memory of the kitchen maid's kindness brings a smile to my face. The descent toward the sea seems steeper than I remembered it. Maybe that's just because I have less strength now than I did then.

As the road makes a sharp bend to the left, I get my first glimpse of Owen's stronghold. Unwilling to be seen until I'm ready to make my request, I take to the woods on the right side of the road and keep making my way downhill, trying to stay a safe distance from the road and make as little noise as possible. When the sentry tower comes in view, I edge deeper into the woods and stop to observe. From what I can tell, the sentries don't seem to be on high alert, instead, talking and laughing among themselves. It occurs to me that there must be enough breeze to waft the sound to me . . . and the direction of the wind means any sound I make will likely be blown away from them. Still, no point in being foolhardy. There might be guards patrolling the woods as well.

Somehow a frontal approach seems unwise, so I decide to skirt the fortress and see if there's anything else I can learn. After all, all I really know about this place is the entrance, the kitchen, and my cell. Reaching the back corner of the side wall, I discover I've found the perfect vantage point to observe the cove and the operation of the fishing fleet. The tide is in and at least half the fleet is already out on the open sea. Two row boats are plying the waters of the cove, taking men from the quay to the waiting boats. Some of the men look robust; others are almost as thin as I am. Owen's conscripts?

A loud noise in the brush behind. I turn, expecting to see an armed guard bearing down on me. Too late to hide . . . and I won't be able to put up much of a fight in my current condition. Then a hawk flies up out of the leaves quite close by, clutching a vole in its talons. I relax and then chuckle to myself. Who'd have ever thought I'd envy a hawk its dinner?

I return my attention to the cove. The last two crews are waiting on the quay for the row boats to return. Most of these men look like conscripts. As I watch, one or two try to break away and make for the woods. The guards use some sort of short whip to drive them back. When one of the row boats returns, the men in charge load this crew first. One man tries to resist and ends up falling into the water. They leave him there, and the row boat goes on its way. When the poor man manages to clamber back up on the quay, the guard pushes him back in the water and points to the fishing boat. It seems the only choice is swim for it or drown.

I'm reminded of Owen's eagerness to buy me from Ralf to work on this fleet. Do I really think there's any hope I could convince Owen to give me passage home? I've nothing to offer him . . . nothing but my labor on his fleet, that is. And how long would he insist I work to earn my passage? Months? Years? Not a faster way home, even assuming I survived. Then another thought comes unbidden: What if Ralf came back here? He and Owen seemed to be friends of some sort. What would Ralf do if he ever saw me again . . . if he discovered I didn't die in that stable? Not something I care to contemplate.

Reluctantly, I turn my back on the cove, make my way deeper into the woods, and begin the long, arduous climb back to the main road.

◆ ◆ ◆ ◆ ◆

It being winter still, there are virtually no travelers abroad. On the rare occasion when I see a rider in the distance, I leave the road and give them a wide berth. There's no predicting someone's reaction to seeing a thin, scruffy man in chains.

Slowly, day by day, I keep plodding eastward. I've started to see the occasional farm at a distance from the roadway. Thinking I might find something to eat, I approach one surreptitiously and am overjoyed when I find a henhouse. Watching for a long time, to assure myself no one is around, I go into the henhouse and check the nests, where I find eggs in abundance. I steal three for each pocket and lope away as quickly as I can to remain undetected. Running isn't possible. That evening, I crack two of the eggs and drink their contents for my supper.

I imagine writing letters to Gwen, telling her I'm coming home . . . telling her I'm traveling as fast as I can to be there for the birth of our child . . . telling her my ideas for names. For a son, I like Geoffrey and Alexander. But royal families are supposed to choose names that pay homage to their ancestors, so I debate with myself how important this might be. For a daughter, I like many names. Eventually, I settle on Margaret Alicia as a tribute to Gwen's mother and to mine.

And thus it goes, day after day, as another full moon passes. I skirt the villages and towns, but whenever I can find shelter near one, I sneak back after dark to look for bits of anything to eat. Once I came across a storage shed that had some sacks of old potatoes. Most were moldy, but I managed to find two that looked like they could still be eaten. Sometimes I go three or four days with nothing to eat but a few acorns.

I'm getting even thinner. My threadbare shirt hangs on my frame and I've had to hitch my trousers up yet again. The soles of my boots are wearing very thin and I know there'll soon be holes in them. But my heart and my head are fixated on home, so I continue walking, knowing not how far I must go or how long it will take me.

◆ ◆ ◆ ◆ ◆

Then the thing I've feared most happens. In the middle of an afternoon, the sky begins to darken early, and I turn to see clouds pushing in quickly from the northwest. Within minutes, the air takes on a chill and the wind begins to blow. A late winter storm is brewing.

I quicken my pace, seeing what looks to be a barn in the far distance. By the time I reach it, the wind is howling, and my blanket is doing little to protect me from the cold. I take a great chance and hurry straight to the barn, hoping that it's open and that no one is there. Luck is with me. The door is unlatched. I open it just enough to get inside and immediately close it against the storm.

My arrival is greeted by a chorus of baa's from a rather large flock of sheep. They're being watched over by two dogs who eye me warily. I stumble over to a corner, make myself a bed of hay, and lie in it, pulling my blanket over me. The dogs decide I'm no threat and return their attention to the sheep as the chorus begins to subside.

As darkness falls and the flock settles down for the night, one of the dogs comes over and sniffs me from head to toe and back again, apparently trying to decide who or what I am. Then he begins nudging vigorously, intent on pushing me aside. "So you want my bed, do you?" I ask him. I lay the blanket aside and get up to gather some more hay, thinking to make another bed for him. He has different ideas, it seems, for when I turn back toward the corner, he's already made himself comfortable in the warm spot I'd vacated. There's nothing for it. I use the hay to make myself a new bed and pull the blanket over me once again. The dog moves close to me, so I let him share the blanket. With the wind still howling outside, I'm grateful for his warmth.

When I wake, the storm has passed and the dog is already back on duty. The sheep are milling around as if anticipating the arrival of someone bringing food. It's then that I notice something I'd missed the night before. Even though it's really too early for lambing season, there – in the middle of the flock – are two tiny lambs huddling close to a ewe. They can't be more than three or four days old. The dogs and the ewe watch me carefully as I approach, but she doesn't flee. Perhaps she senses my hunger, for she stands quietly and lets me milk her. I capture the precious liquid in my cupped hand and drink it greedily, but I know I have to leave some for the lambs.

I'm half tempted to wait for the herdsman and try to convince him to help me. It wouldn't be easy. I have none of his language and he'll have none of mine. More likely, he'll be frightened by finding me here in the barn and might even sic the dogs on me. The one that slept with me might leave me alone, but I doubt the other one would be so generous. It isn't worth the risk, so I wrap my blanket around me, open the door, and turn my steps east yet again.

◆ ◆ ◆ ◆ ◆

I plod on, grateful for those rare days when I find a henhouse unattended or a handful of oats left in a feeder in a barn. The expected holes have appeared in the soles of my boots. The sun is starting to break winter's chill, and from time to time I see a tree showing that faintly fuzzy look that means the imminent emergence of young buds.

One afternoon, it begins to rain . . . just a light sprinkle, but as there's no sign of a break in the clouds, I'm relieved to see a ramshackle building not too far from the road. Approaching it, I discover just how neglected it is. The roof is intact over one corner, but the rest is rotting and parts of it have fallen in. There's a bench of some sort in the roofed corner. It's unclear if it will hold the weight of a man; but as it seems the only dry spot available, I clamber up onto it. Luck is with me once again, for though it creaks, it doesn't fall.

It rains steadily for three days. I venture out once each day to cup my hands and collect rainwater to drink, leaving my blanket on the bench so that it doesn't get wet. And each time, when I come back in soaked and shivering, I have to struggle with myself not to wrap it around me until I've dried out.

When the sun returns to the sky, I return to the road. But with no food these past three days, I'm growing weaker of body, and I can sense that is having an effect on my strength of mind. Remember the child, I remind myself. Your child needs a father. You've no choice but to keep going.

◆ ◆ ◆ ◆ ◆

The neat stubble on the right side of the road left from the previous year's harvest of wheat has given way to hay fields – scraggly and unkempt looking, just waiting for spring to return. Surprisingly, this lifts my spirits; seeing a change in the landscape makes it easier to believe I'm actually making progress on my journey. Late one afternoon I spot a mass of banners in the distance. From the number of them and the fact that they don't seem to be moving, I surmise there must be a large army encamped. The distance is too great for me to discern the markings on the banners . . . and it's unlikely I'd recognize any of them in this part of the world anyway . . . so I turn my attention to finding a place to hide should they advance in my direction. A small grove of trees is the best I can do, but it seems to provide sufficient cover, and there are a few scattered acorns around to eat. I make a bed of fallen leaves and settle down for the night.

In the morning, the army is gone. I can't imagine how such a large force could have departed without my hearing the sounds of horses and wagons and shouted orders; but there's not a banner in sight. There are likely, however, to be scraps of food left behind. As I approach where I remember seeing the banners, some low farm buildings come into view. I drop to the ground to watch for any sign of people and see a woman emerge from one of the buildings carrying a large basket. She crosses the yard and begins hanging the contents of the basket across a line strung between two posts. My banners, it seems, were nothing more than the family washing, drying in the breeze. I remember hearing it said that when a man is starving, he often sees things that aren't there. What I saw was really there, but the reality was not what I thought I saw.

When the woman retreats inside, I venture closer and manage to grab two precious eggs from the henhouse before I hear the stirring of people again. In my haste to get away, I trip over a small rock and fall to the ground, breaking one of my eggs. There's nothing for it . . . I must go on with my single remaining egg, for the activity on the farm is increasing, and I've no wish to be seen.

◆ ◆ ◆ ◆ ◆

I pass a walled town with a fortress in the center and think it looks like the town where my ordeal first began. Am I hallucinating or is it real? And if it's real, is it really the same town or just another of the walled towns in the Territories that so often look quite similar? I keep walking, but I'm covering fewer and fewer miles each day and finding less and less to eat.

Tonight, as I gaze at another full moon, I wonder how much longer I can go on. I'd found another henhouse today and stolen the only two eggs that were there. As I drink them for my supper, I wonder if they have any power to restore a modicum of strength. I sleep fitfully, reliving the raid on the camp over and over in my dreams.

When morning comes, I look at the road before me and wonder if there's any point in going on. There's nothing in sight in any direction . . . nothing to tell me where I am or how much farther I have to go. No sign of any food or water. No trees where the animals might have left a stray acorn or two. Perhaps Ralf was right after all. Perhaps he did take me so far from home that there's no way to return. Perhaps it's my fate to die here alone without ever having seen my child. I tell myself I must try one day more before giving in to despair.

Around midday, I see a village ahead. It seems to be bustling with all manner of activity—perhaps a market day. I give the village a wide berth, my mouth salivating at the thought of the food I might find at a market, but my mind telling me that good village people would turn away from me in fright . . . might even do me harm . . . though what more harm could be done to me, I really can't imagine.

As I return to the road, I see in the distance a building that looks something like a monastery. Through the fog of my mind, I begin to remember things. A village, a nearby monastery . . . landmarks that indicate the border of our kingdom with the Territories.

Could this be possible? Could it be that I've made it . . . that I'm home at last?

I try to run toward the monastery but can only manage a feeble shuffle. It seems so far away. What if the gate is shut and locked? What if no one is there? What if it isn't the place I think it to be after all?

At long last, I shuffle up the path to the gates. I realize I'm crying — tears of relief and joy as I see the open gates and take the last feeble steps through them. My heart sinks when I see there's no one in the courtyard, and now I'm crying tears of true despair.

Then a monk comes around the corner of the chapel. He sees me and begins running toward me, calling to others for help as he runs. I cannot take another step. I simply stand there, and when he arrives, I collapse into his arms.

They carry me into a small room, which I assume must be a monk's cell, and lay me on a bed that some might say was hard but is the softest bed I've known in months. The monk who found me is giving orders. "Fetch Brother Infirmerer and the Prior. And bring some warm broth and bread from the kitchen."

He covers me with a clean blanket and sits in a chair beside me. "I am Brother Warin," he says. "You're safe here. We will care for you, and when you've recovered some, perhaps you can tell us who you are and how you came to be in this dreadful state."

For the moment, I don't have the strength to respond. All I can do is grasp his hand and give it a feeble squeeze. The door opens and two monks enter, one bearing a tray and the other carrying a box.

"Ah, Brother Infirmerer," says Brother Warin. "I'm grateful for your presence. This man needs much attention."

The infirmerer looks at me and says, "What this man needs first is food," and he stands aside to let the monk with the tray approach. The tray contains a bowl filled with steaming liquid and a big hunk of bread.

"Slowly," cautions the infirmerer. "We don't know when he last ate or what his stomach can handle. Dip small morsels of bread in the broth and let him eat those . . . very slowly. We'll see how he fares and then determine what to do next."

The broth-soaked bread tastes like manna from heaven, but I can only manage five or six bites, so shrunken is my stomach from weeks of deprivation.

"Don't worry that you can't eat much at first," says the infirmerer. "This is the normal way that our bodies recover from starvation. Eat a bit more whenever you feel hungry. You'll be surprised how quickly you become absolutely ravenous and are demanding to eat everything in our larder."

I manage to utter a quiet, "Thank you."

"When you've recovered a bit of strength, we'll get you cleaned up and out of these irons and see what medicines," he gestures to his box, "you need."

The door opens and another monk enters. From his air of authority and the deference the others show to him, I know this is the prior. Brother Warin rises from the chair, relinquishing it to his superior.

"I am Prior André, my son," he says.

The name seems somehow familiar.

"Part of our mission here is to help refugees from the Territories."

When he says this I know for certain. I've crossed the border into our kingdom. I'm home. My elation is enough to give me the strength to speak.

"I'm no refugee, Prior. I'm Alfred, son of Lord Edward."

The prior seems taken aback, but quickly recovers his composure. "We'll care for you, my son. Do not fret. My Brother Infirmerer tells me what you need now is rest and food."

He rises and beckons to Brother Warin to follow him. I overhear him say, "Send to Ernle at once. I think I know him, but it's been too many years. If this man is who he says he is, Ernle will know and will know what to do."

I doze for a bit. When I wake there's a monk sitting in the chair ready to give me more broth-soaked bread. I manage a few more morsels and ask for some water. And then I doze again.

I wake to the commotion of rapid footsteps in the corridor, and the door is thrown open. I recognize Lord Ernle and try to rise on my elbows to greet him.

"My God, Alfred, it *is* you," he exclaims. "I hardly dared to hope." He sits in the chair and takes my hand, sees the extent of my shackles, and flings off my blanket to reveal the rest. "My God, lad, who's done this to you? No, no . . . don't try to answer now. There'll be time enough for that."

Then he turns to the prior and starts issuing orders. "I trust you have a wagon we can use. We need to get him to the manor so my blacksmith can remove those chains."

Nothing seems to disturb the prior's equanimity. "Let him stay here overnight, Lord Ernle. We need to get some food in him to begin restoring his strength. I agree we need to get the shackles off, and we have no ability to do that here. But one more night won't harm him further. Tomorrow I'll send him to you; and I'll send Brother Infirmerer along to tend his wounds and supervise his restoration to health."

"Yes, of course," says Ernle. "That makes sense. I'll get home and send word to the castle right away. Take care of him, André. We must get him home safely."

And then they're all gone—all except for the monk who's assigned to attend me.

I lose track of whether it's day or night. I sleep for a while. When I wake, my attendant is there in case I need anything. Once I drink quite a bit of broth. He won't let me have it all, and I trust he knows best.

The next time I wake, a different monk is in attendance. "Ah, good morning," he says cheerfully. "Welcome back to the land of the living."

I feel surprisingly refreshed, but I haven't yet tried to sit or stand. He helps me to sit up on the edge of the bed. "There's a bucket in the corner for you to relieve yourself. Can you manage on your own or do you need my help?"

"Let me try," I reply. I manage reasonably well and return to sit on the bed. He opens the door and calls for a brother to bring something to break my fast. In a few minutes, another monk appears with a small bowl of steaming porridge.

"Now don't eat it all at once," my attendant admonishes. "A few bites, slow and easy at first. Take your time."

I follow his instructions. In a while, I've eaten almost half the bowl and feel quite satiated.

"That's good," says the monk. "Enough for now." And he sets the bowl aside.

Prior André arrives, accompanied by the infirmerer. "You look somewhat better this morning," he remarks. "Do you think you could tolerate the ride to Ernle's manor?"

"I'd like to try." My voice is definitely stronger than it was yesterday.

"In that case, the wagon is ready. It's not such a long journey. I think you look fit enough to travel that far. What say you, Brother Infirmerer?"

"I agree, sir. I think we should be on our way."

"A moment, Prior," I say. "Yesterday I heard you say you thought you knew me. And I've been thinking that possibly I know you as well. Certainly I know your name."

"I wondered if you'd remember. I served under Abbot Francis and was your tutor for a time when you were a boy. Francis sent me here seven years ago to lead this place and to help the migrants from the Territories."

He extends his arms and I rise to accept his embrace.

"God be with you, Alfred, as he most surely has been to bring you back to us."

"Thank you," I reply, "for being here to be my salvation."

"That is what we do, my son."

The infirmerer gives me a cloak to wrap around me both for warmth and to hide my chains. He then extends his arm, and I use it to steady myself as we walk out to where the wagon is waiting. I can already feel the restorative effects of food, for I feel ever so slightly stronger than the last time I was on my feet.

The sun is shining and the air feels almost warm. As we drive through the gate and pull up in front of the manor house, Ernle is rushing from the door to greet us. "Alfred, my boy, you still look frightful, but I must admit you're a bit less ghostly than when I saw you yesterday." I smile at his attempt at levity.

"The blacksmith says it won't all be pleasant, but he can definitely free you from your chains. He's ready whenever you are."

"The sooner the better," I reply.

"Is he up to it, Brother Infirmerer?"

"I believe we should let him be the judge of that," replies the monk. "Being free of those shackles will do as much for his spirit as a mountain of food will do for his body."

"Then let's go." Ernle climbs up into the wagon. "Follow that path. The smithy is right next to the stable. My stable boys can help you with your horse and wagon while the blacksmith goes to work."

When I remove my cloak at the smithy, the blacksmith gasps. "My God, m'lord, who did this t'ye? No self-respecting blacksmith would ever let himself be used to do this to a man."

"All in good time, Fulk," chides Ernle. "Let's get him free."

It takes quite some time, but eventually Fulk gets me free of all the relics of my captivity. He's about to throw it all into the forge to melt it down when I say, "Wait! I want to keep one of the wrist bands." They all look at me as if I've taken leave of my senses. "I don't ever want to forget the extent of cruelty that can exist in a man. I doubt I ever shall, but I'd like to have a symbol to pass on to my children and my children's children so that they, too, never forget."

The monk, Lord Ernle, and I then walk slowly back to the manor house. "We've made a room ready for you so you can rest and recover," says Ernle. "And my squire has found you some clothes. You're so thin, he had trouble finding something that might fit right, but he did his best."

"Thank you," I reply, "but what I want now more than anything in the world is a hot bath with lots of soap, followed by a haircut and a shave."

The infirmerer speaks up. "Best make that a warm bath. Getting in water too hot in your weakened state would make you weaker still."

"Alright, then," I say, "a warm bath. But with lots of soap."

The infirmerer laughs. "But before you get in that bath, I want to look at those sores on your wrists and neck and see what condition your feet are in after being in those boots for so many months."

"My squire is at your service, Alfred, as long as you're here," says Ernle.

We've arrived at the house. The few steps up to the entry tire me. Inside, I take one look at the staircase and grimace.

"Don't fret, son," says Ernle. "We'll help you. And we can go as slowly as you like."

It's a long, slow climb, and I'm exhausted when we reach the top of the stairs. Fortunately, my room is the first door off the corridor. The squire is waiting inside. Ernle closes the door behind him as he leaves us.

"Why don't ye sit, m'lord, and let me be getting those clothes and boots off ye."

"The only place I'm fit to sit right now . . . " I hesitate, not knowing his name.

"Thomas, m'lord."

"The only place I'm fit to sit right now, Thomas, is a wooden stool, if you have one."

"I do, m'lord, in the dressing room. Just beside yer bath."

I let him undress me. Removing my boots proves to be a bit of a bother, but he gets it done and then removes my stockings and trousers. I catch a glimpse of myself in the mirror and gasp involuntarily. I'm emaciated and filthy, with the hair and beard of a wild man.

"Sit," orders the infirmerer, and when I comply, he begins examining my feet. I look down. The toenails have indeed grown quite long and have turned yellow and black.

"As I suspected. Toenail rot," pronounces the infirmerer. "Thomas, fetch us some vinegar."

While Thomas is gone, the monk retrieves some scissors from his box and cuts my toenails to a respectable length. Next, he looks at my hands and uses the scissors to even up the rough mess I'd made chewing off my finger nails. Then he examines the sores on my wrists and neck.

"It's bad," he pronounces, "but not as bad as I would have thought."

So I tell him about the kitchen maid and her salve and the partial healing it had brought about midway through my ordeal.

"There'll likely be some scars," he says, "but nothing like what there would have been if not for your kitchen maid."

Thomas returns with a pitcher of vinegar and a basin. "Hold your feet over the basin," orders the monk; and he pours the vinegar all over my feet. "You must do this morning and night for a month and then once a day until the nails are back to their normal pink color. Your feet may smell like pickles for a while, but they will be cured.

"Now into the bath with you. Thomas, let's get him clean."

The water and soap feel heavenly. The soap is painful on my wounds, but the monk insists it's essential to get them clean. When they've scrubbed me from head to toe, Thomas makes me stand up in the tub. He pours pitchers of warm water over me to rinse away the last of the soap and grime. When I step out of the bath, I feel almost human again.

The vinegar is poured over my feet again, and then Thomas dresses me in clean clothes for the first time in months. Unsurprisingly, they're too big; but Thomas manages to make adjustments so they don't fall off. The feeling is luxurious. "No stockings or boots for a few days," says the monk. "Slippers only. Those feet need air. Now let's dress those sores."

He puts a salve all over my raw skin and wraps each wrist and my neck in soft cloth. "Fresh dressings every day, Thomas," he says. "We should keep them wrapped for at least a week. After that, they'll benefit from the air. But keep applying the salve until they're completely healed. I'll leave you extra pots of it."

Seated on the stool again, I let Thomas cut my hair. When he produces a razor to give me a shave, the monk stops him. "Let's just trim it short and neat for now. His skin is probably not up to a razor yet. Once you have your strength back and have started to put on some weight . . . then we'll know that your body is starting to heal and your skin can tolerate the assault of sharpened steel."

When Thomas has finished with me, I assess myself in the mirror. A totally different man from the one who walked into this dressing room less than an hour ago.

I walk into the bedchamber and sit in a chair. It's softer than I can imagine a chair could ever be. There's a knock at the door, and Thomas runs to open it. He takes a tray from a kitchen maid and sets it on the low table in front of me. A bowl of broth, some bread, and a glass about one-third full of wine.

"Perfect," says the monk. "Porridge, broth, and bread for the next couple of days. And a little bit of wine once a day will do him good. After that, we can add a bit of meat and some potato and slowly get him back to a regular diet. I'll stay here for a few days just to watch and be sure he has no other ill effects from his ordeal. Now eat . . . rest . . . and I'll be back to check on you from time to time."

As he leaves, Ernle enters. "Now that looks more like the Alfred I know," he says, seating himself in the chair opposite me. "I sent a courier riding hard to the castle yesterday afternoon. He should arrive by tomorrow night. No doubt they'll send for you right away. In the meantime, let's see what we can do about restoring your strength. Eat and rest this afternoon. My wife and I will have supper in our chamber this evening and would be honored if you'd have your broth with us. We won't ask you to try the stairs again today." He smiles. "I'm going to leave Thomas here with you. Anything you want, just ask him. Anything at all."

"Thank you, sir. I'd be very grateful for the company at supper tonight. It's been many weeks since I've had human companionship."

After he leaves, I eat and then nap. The bed is delightfully soft with piles of pillows to cushion my head. It seems a different lifetime when I was ever so comfortable.

I find myself hungrier and hungrier each day, eating a little more at each meal. I walk around the manor to start rebuilding my strength. The stairs are still the most tiring, but I must climb them at the end of every day. The first time I tried to raise my arms, I couldn't get them above the level of my shoulders. This was quite alarming, but Brother Infirmerer assured me it was normal. "Your body has learned different habits while you were chained," he explained. "It will take time for it to relearn the former patterns of use. Keep trying. A little higher each day. It will be difficult or even painful at first, but your body will learn. If you're diligent about this, I predict you'll be nearly back to normal within a month."

The meat and potato have been added to my diet, and the monk now says it's safe for me to eat as much as I want. Lord Ernle has a small library, and I've found a book to read to exercise my mind.

Over supper in the evenings, I've been telling my story to Lord and Lady Ernle. They seem in awe of how I managed to survive. When I explain that it was the thought of my child that kept me going, they look at each other knowingly. I don't think to ask them about that, because I suddenly realize that they're the first people I've told that I'm to be a father.

Brother Infirmerer checks on me every day, asking questions about my eating, my exercise, my bowels . . . checking my dressings to be sure Thomas has done it right . . . looking for any sign that I may have some latent illness or injury. On the fifth day, he pronounces himself satisfied that I'm on the road to recovery and announces that he'll depart the following morning.

I'm feeling stronger every day and am now permitted boots when I go outside. I walk down to the smithy to see Fulk and thank him again for freeing me from captivity. When he sees me, he roars, "M'lord, just look at ye! I'd never know ye be the same man if I dinna' see it with me own eyes. Ye'll be yerself in no time, that's fer sure."

I walk over to the stable and visit the horses. Stroking their big heads and seeing how they respond is therapeutic in a way I never would have imagined. I begin to believe Fulk is right—I will be myself again sometime soon.

I hear someone calling my name and turn to see Thomas running toward the stable at full tilt. "Lord Alfred! Sir! Ye best come! Come quick! There be something ye should see."

Quick is relative for me, but I do my best to follow him as quickly as I can. As we round the corner of the house, he points up the lane. "Look . . . there."

A troop of horsemen is riding down the lane toward the manor. As they get closer, I recognize the king's banner. And as they ride up to the house, I realize it's a troop of the King's Own Guard with

Samuel in command. My eyes fill with tears at the sight of my old friend.

He halts his troop properly, then jumps from his horse and runs to me, embracing me in a great bear hug. I cling to him as to life itself. After a moment, he pushes me away and appraises me from head to toe. "My God, Alfred." This is becoming my standard greeting, it seems. "You look . . . " He stops. I think he might have been about to say "like hell" and thought better of it.

"Actually, somewhat better than I feared." Lord Ernle has come out the entrance and is dashing down the steps to embrace his son.

Samuel continues. "From what the courier told us, it sounded like you were a ghost in chains."

"That he was," chimes in Lord Ernle. "But he's started on the road back."

"Thanks to your father, his blacksmith, his squire, and some very special monks," I tell Samuel.

Samuel suddenly remembers his duties and turns to his troop. "Troop, dis-mount!" he orders. "Thomas, would you be so kind as to show the men to the stable and arrange quarters for them?"

Thomas is pleased to be asked. "This way, sirs," he beckons.

"Oh, by the way," Samuel turns back to me. "I brought you something." And at that moment the last knight approaches, leading two horses, one of them Star Dancer. I take his lead and Star Dancer nuzzles me as if I'd never been away. Samuel reaches into his pouch and tosses me an apple. "Thought you might not have one of these."

I give Star Dancer the apple, and we walk with Samuel and his mount down to where the grooms are settling the horses in.

Our walk back to the house is slow. I've had more exertion in the last hour than in previous days. Talking with Samuel, it finally seems real to me that life will, indeed, become normal again.

"Tell me about Gwen," I implore him. "Is she alright? Has the baby come?"

Reaching into his waistcoat, he produces a folded paper and hands it to me. I stop in my tracks and unfold it quickly.

My dearest darling Alfred,

The messenger just arrived, and I write this in haste as Samuel is leaving within the hour. I never gave up hope. I always felt you were alive out there somewhere. And now to know for certain, it fills my heart almost to bursting. Come home to me, my love, as soon as you can.

"She says nothing about the baby."

"She said to tell you that all is well and that you're not to worry."

"Come on, Samuel, you know how much I love her. The thought of that baby is what's kept me going all these months."

"My friend," he says, "it's not worth my life to disobey that lady's instructions. 'All is well.' She gave me strict orders—that's all I'm permitted to tell you." He pauses and claps me on the shoulder. "Trust me, Alfred. All is very well indeed."

It's been just over a week since I stumbled into the monastery, and I marvel at how far I've come in such a short time. I'm still exceedingly thin, there's as yet no visible progress in the healing of my feet, and I still tire quite easily.

When Thomas hears me stirring, he enters from the dressing room carrying my bowl of morning porridge. I know not how Lord Ernle is coping without the services of his squire, but I'll be forever grateful to him for the loan of Thomas. He fusses over me like a mother hen, makes sure I eat and rest properly, attends to my maladies, and has made it possible for me to start recovering my strength.

Samuel is a tonic for my spirits — a tangible connection to my home and my life there. I feel a new urgency this morning to finish my journey — to be well and truly home.

As I'm buttoning my trousers, there's a knock on the door and I call, "Come!" Samuel enters and makes his way into the dressing room, where Thomas is preparing to treat my feet.

"My God, Alfred," that greeting again. "What happened to your feet?"

"Comes from not taking your boots off for half a year," I reply. As I hold my feet over the basin and Thomas pours the vinegar, I add, "But Brother Infirmerer assures me that if I keep pickling them in this stuff, they'll eventually come right again."

The dressings aren't yet on my wrists or neck — I remove them for my bath so we can clean the wounds carefully. Samuel comes over and takes my hands, turning them over and over to look carefully at my wrists. Then he lifts my chin to look at my neck.

"Your grandfather wants a full report. I think he suspects you might want to keep the worst from him."

"In that, he would be correct."

"Father's told me what shape you were in when you arrived. This looks like you're starting to heal."

"I am. Thanks to the infirmerer's salve and Thomas's ministrations." Thomas is now busily applying the salve and dressings.

"The infirmerer said you could start leaving the dressings off soon, m'lord," Thomas reminds me, "for the skin to get some air."

"Right, Thomas, but I think I'll let people see the dressings first before they have to look at the healing sores."

Then I turn to my friend. "Samuel, I want to go home . . . now."

"Do you think you're up to it? Can you ride?"

"Likely not at our usual pace. But my legs are fairly strong. I think I can sit a horse. The only problem is going to be mounting and dismounting. I still can't raise my arms much above my shoulders. I try every day and Thomas is helping me." We demonstrate how I raise my arms, try to force them higher, and then Thomas gently tries to push them just a little higher still.

"We're making progress, but it's slow. I doubt I'll be able to reach Star Dancer's withers, and I certainly won't be able to pull myself into the saddle. I'll need a stool or mounting block for sure."

"Very well," says Samuel. "But I want to see what you're capable of before I agree to take you away from here on such a journey. Thomas, run down to the stable and ask them to saddle my horse and Star Dancer. We'll be down shortly so I can see what our lad can do." And Thomas is off to do Samuel's bidding.

"Well, if I'm going to ride, I suppose boots are in order," I say.

"If I think you're fit enough," says Samuel, "we'll go this afternoon. I think half a day in the saddle is enough for your first try. And there's a town half a day's ride from here where we can spend the night. We'll stay in the towns so we have decent food and shelter — no camping in the open for you in your current state."

My boots on, I stand ready for my first real test. "I'll agree to that. Now let's go see if I can still ride a horse."

We arrive at the stable to find both horses ready and a mounting block in place for me. I support myself on Samuel's shoulder to step up on the block, and he stands ready to help me as I place my left foot in the stirrup and swing my right leg over. It's an effort, but at least I don't fall.

I reach for the reins and pat Star Dancer's neck. "Take care of me, old friend," I tell him.

Samuel mounts and we walk out of the stable yard and up the path toward the house. "Nothing more than a walk for now," he says, and I gladly comply.

Riding uses the legs in a very different way from walking, and I quickly realize the wisdom of Samuel's plan for a short first day in the saddle. We make a couple of circuits of the lawn in front of the manor and then go back down to the stable.

A groom pulls the mounting block up beside Star Dancer. Samuel dismounts and moves quickly to assist me as I think about how I should attempt this. Finally, I swing my right leg over Star Dancer's neck and slide down his side onto the block, using Samuel's shoulder for support.

The grooms cheer, and Samuel says, "Well, at least he didn't fall off."

Then he turns to me. "What do you think?"

"I think I want to go home."

"Then let's go back up to the house and get ready to do just that." He claps me on the shoulder then turns and calls to Thomas, who quickly catches us up.

"Thomas," he starts issuing orders. "If you will. Find Sir Nigel. Tell him to get the mounts and troops ready. We'll leave after the midday meal. Then help Alfred here pack his things."

I interrupt him. "I have no things, remember? Just the clothes on my back."

"Find him a spare clean shirt, Thomas. And some more clean stockings. We don't want those feet to get any worse. Put them in my pack. I don't want him carrying any extra weight. Then see if you can find him a coat . . . or better still, a woolen cloak. It's still not fully spring, and we could have a cool or cloudy day easily enough.

"Put his medicines and cloth for the dressings in my pack, too. I'll help him with changing them."

"And Thomas," I interrupt again. "Please don't forget my shackle."

"What about the vinegar, m'lord? For his feet."

"I think we'll be able to find some vinegar in the tavern or somewhere in each town. But put a flask of brandy in my pack, too. Just in case anything should happen on the road.

"Off with you then," he says to Thomas and turning to me, "Let's go find Father and tell him our plan. Then you should rest before we eat."

Lord Ernle is apprehensive and tries to convince me to wait a few more days before undertaking the trip. "You may very well be right, sir," I tell him. "But I'm aching to be home. Samuel will get me there safely."

Lord Ernle looks at his son. "See that you do," he admonishes . . . and then smiles to let us know that he has absolute confidence in his son.

"Sir, there is no way I can properly thank you for what you've done for me," I say, struggling to keep my emotions in check.

"It's nothing you or your father wouldn't have done for my Samuel," he replies. "I'll send a courier to the castle to tell them of your plans. They'll be anxious to know something, I'm sure."

I leave father and son alone and return to my chamber to rest for the journey. It hardly seems real.

We depart after the midday meal. Samuel invites me to ride in the lead alongside him. He makes this appear to his troop like he's doing me honor, but I'm fairly certain he just wants to keep an eye on me. And for that, I'm grateful.

The standard bearer follows behind us and then the rest of the troop. As we start up the lane from the manor, I have another surprise. The knight riding behind me brings out another standard — my own. I'm overwhelmed. I reach out to Samuel and grasp his hand in a brief gesture of gratitude.

We stop in the town as the sun is beginning to set. The tavern has rooms for about half of us; the remainder of the knights will sleep in the stable. Supper is a hearty stew with meat, potatoes, and onions. I have a bit of ale . . . the first in many months . . . and find it both tasty and restorative.

Exhausted, I fall asleep immediately and don't wake until Samuel shakes my shoulder. He's found a bowl of porridge and some vinegar, and he sets about treating my feet while I eat. We change my dressings and are ready to be on our way. In the stable, the knights are already mounted and ready to go, and our horses are saddled and waiting.

Once out on the road, Samuel sends one of his men ahead as a courier to carry the message of our progress. "Cedric would chide you for reducing your troop strength," I tease him.

He gets into the spirit of it right away. "Ah, but the final responsibility for the disposition and dispersal of the troops rests with the captain. And that, my good man, just happens to be me."

We laugh together. "How is the old man?" I ask.

"Not well, Alfred. His health gets no better. The winter cold did him no favors either."

Because of our pace and our plan to stay only in the towns it will take us four more days to reach the castle rather than the usual three. We also stop longer than usual at midday to allow me some rest. At the end of the first full day, I'm more tired than I could have believed possible, and my legs are sore from the unfamiliar use in riding. But my stamina and the soreness start to improve as we ride on. Each day, Samuel sends another courier.

As we ride, Samuel gets me to tell him about my ordeal. I find myself telling him details that I'd be unwilling to share with anyone else, even to telling him how nearly I came to giving up one day too soon. He listens attentively, encouraging me to continue whenever I go quiet for a bit, somehow knowing that I need to talk about it before I can really start to heal.

On the morning of the day we're to arrive at the castle, I share with him my apprehension about dismounting on arrival. "I don't want to make a fool of myself, Samuel, or look more feeble than I am."

"Don't worry, my friend. I've got that all worked out." He'll say no more, so I simply have to trust him.

My heart is in my throat when we catch the first glimpse of the castle on the horizon. I'm able to regain my composure as we draw nearer and nearer and the image is not so new.

Someone must have posted a lookout, because the church bells start to ring as we enter the town. People are cheering in the streets as we pass, and I'm awed and honored by this outpouring of goodwill.

Samuel slows our pace as we arrive at the castle gates. "Are you ready?"

I reach out and grasp his hand. "This is a good day, my friend. Thank you for bringing me home." We resume our pace and enter the castle grounds.

Again, I'm awed. On the right side of the courtyard assembled at attention are the remainder of the King's Own Guard and two troops of knights. Samuel circles our procession around to the left, and I immediately see what he has planned.

On each side of the steps leading to the entrance is a low wall as high as a man's thigh and wide enough to walk on. Someone walking on the wall can move directly onto the third or fourth step quite easily—we did it all the time as boys.

Samuel brings the troop around and halts with Star Dancer next to the wall. To those not in the know, it might appear he hasn't given me room to dismount, but it's perfect. The wall is high enough that I can use Star Dancer's back to support myself even with my limited arm movement.

Samuel and I both dismount. The king, my parents, and Harold are all at the top of the steps. As I make my way across the wall, Samuel bounds up the steps and bows to the king.

"Your Grace," he says, "it's my happy duty to report that we have fulfilled your orders."

"Well done, Captain," he says loud enough for all in the courtyard to hear. And then he does something quite extraordinary. He goes down to where Samuel is standing and embraces him for a long moment. "Very well done, indeed, Samuel. I have no words to thank you enough."

I'm making my way slowly up the steps as Samuel moves aside and the king resumes his position. The anxiety in my heart must be visible on my face, for as I reach the top step, the others move aside, and there's Gwen holding a bundle in her arms.

I'm overwhelmed with emotion and can't control the tears flowing from my eyes as I go to her. My beautiful Gwen—more beautiful at this moment than I have ever seen her.

She holds the bundle so I can see the tiny baby. "Meet your daughter, my love. She came to us two weeks earlier that we expected and is five weeks old today."

I cannot find words. I touch the baby's cheek gently and put an arm around Gwen. Finally, I manage, "She's beautiful. Just like her mother."

Gwen gives me the baby, saying, "Juliana, meet your father." I take her . . . awkwardly at first, and then slowly figure out how to hold her. Gwen puts her arm around me and leads me toward the door as the others follow.

Inside, with the doors closed to give us some privacy, Gwen takes the baby back so I can greet the others. I go to my mother first and she hugs me closely. "My God, Alfred!"

I can't help myself. I'm laughing out loud. Mother looks totally perplexed. "Have I said something wrong, Alfred? It's just that you're so dreadfully thin."

"Nothing wrong, Mother," I reassure her, hugging her again. "Nothing at all. It's just that I've grown so accustomed to hearing that phrase whenever people first see me that I've begun to think of it as my own personal greeting."

The tension of my homecoming broken, I go to embrace my father. "Welcome home, Son. It matters not how thin you are . . . only that you're here."

I turn next to Harold. As we break our embrace, I say to him, "Perhaps now I can finally fulfill that dining invitation I made to you so long ago."

He grins. "Nothing would please me more, Alfred."

I've saved my grandfather for last. "Grandfather," is all I can say. Our embrace lasts a very long time. He seems much more frail than when I saw him last. Though it's been less than a year, he seems to have aged ten years or more. I'll have to speak with my father about it.

Finally, he breaks the embrace, pats me on the back, and says, "Tonight you spend with your family. Get to know your little Juliana. My Juliana would have been very proud of her—and of you. But come to me in the morning when you're ready. I want to hear everything, and there's much I want to tell you."

I return to Gwen and my daughter. As we all walk down the corridor, Gwen says, "Your parents thought it best that we go ahead and have her christened; and eventually I agreed they were right."

"Of course they were," I reassure her.

"I named her Juliana Jehanne—for our grandmothers."

"It's a beautiful name. I can think of none finer."

She turns toward my grandfather. "I think there's someone else here who quite agrees with you."

My grandfather is beaming with pleasure. I'm amazed. Over the vast expanse of time and separation, Gwen and I had both arrived at the same idea. We'd just chosen different generations of grandmothers.

We reach the staircase, and I look up at it with a bit of dread. Stairs are getting easier, but it's been a long, emotional day. I start to climb slowly, using conversation with the others as my disguise.

My father, always observant, realizes what I'm doing, comes to my side, and offers me his arm, which I gladly accept. "There's no shame in admitting your strength isn't fully restored yet, Son. And it's good for all of us to be able to help you."

As we reach the top of the stairs, Mother says, "We've made arrangements for you and Gwen to have supper with us tonight . . . to help Gwen, as she's been so busy with the baby. Are you up to it?"

"Of course, Mother. The monk who cared for me in the first days said I would get to a point where I was ravenously hungry, and he was right. I still can't eat a lot at any one time, but I'm very hungry after a long day riding."

"Are there things you should or shouldn't eat?" asks my mother. "Or something you particularly want?"

"Nothing too rich just yet. Simple food is still best for the next week or two. But I'm sure anything from our kitchens will be delicious."

It's then that I recognize what's happening. Someone has understood that I need time to adjust to being in these surroundings before I have to bare my body and soul to Gwen. I see Father's fine hand in this . . . and perhaps Gwen's as well . . . and realize that the best way to thank them is simply to accept their generosity.

We go to my parents' quarters, my mother gives some orders to her maid, and we settle in to talk while we wait for the supper. I tell them about my time at Ernle's and the wonderful people who took care of me there.

Juliana begins to whimper and fret. "Excuse me," says Gwen. "She's hungry." And she takes the baby into my parents' bed chamber.

My mother tilts her head in the direction of the bed chamber, indicating I should follow. I watch as Gwen bares her breast and begins to feed the baby. "I decided to nurse her myself," she says, "rather than find a wet nurse." She looks at me with a bit of apprehension. "I spoke with your mother about it, and she very much approved. I hope you don't mind."

"Why should I mind?" I ask.

"So many men want their wives back to normal and the baby out of sight."

"Do you think I'm that kind of man?"

"No . . . that's why I took the chance."

I go to her, kiss her on top of the head, and leave her to feed Juliana. They rejoin us as the food is brought in and laid on the sideboard.

Over supper, I ask about my grandfather's health. "He seems so frail compared to the last time I saw him."

"There's no question about it, Alfred," answers my father. "The past six months have been very hard on him. When you were first taken, he moved heaven and earth to try to discover where you were. We heard rumors of a ransom being asked, but no specific demand ever arrived here.

"Then Abbot Francis passed into the next world. Losing his friend was a real blow, even though he'd known Francis was in ill health for some time.

"And the longer you were gone, the more he blamed himself for sending you there and putting you in harm's way. More than once he said to me, 'If Alfred is lost to us, I've no one to blame but myself.' His remorse over your fate has weighed very heavily on him."

He pauses long enough to replenish my wine glass.

"You should have seen him when Ernle's messenger arrived. His heart visibly lightened, and I actually think I saw him stand a bit taller. Each day, when Samuel's couriers arrived, I could see the years start to fall away. I doubt he'll completely get back his old vitality, but perhaps you and he can recover some of your strength together."

He pauses thoughtfully for a long moment. "There's someone else who's been deeply affected by all this."

I look at him quizzically.

"Harold. He told us that it was you who shot Ranulf and saved his life. He also told us that he saw you being taken and, though he ran, he couldn't get there fast enough to intervene. He's been chastising himself all these months for not being able to prevent your capture."

"It was no one's fault," I say. "All was confusion and chaos, and everyone was just trying to do whatever they could. I blame no one."

"You have a more generous spirit than many men might, Alfred. Perhaps you can find a way to help Harold come to peace with what he perceives to be his guilt."

"That I shall."

Supper is finished, and it's time. "I still get tired easily, and it's been a long day. Mother . . . Father . . . will you excuse us for the night?"

Gwen rises and takes my hand. Mother stands and kisses me on the cheek. "I must have done a really good job," she says with a smile on her face. "I see nothing's been able to spoil your good manners."

As we enter our chamber, Gwen says, "There's someone here who's been waiting all day to see you."

I walk in to find Osbert there and quickly move to embrace my loyal squire. I see the tears in his eyes and speak quickly to spare him embarrassment. "So many times, Osbert, I wondered if you'd gotten caught up in that raid."

"Nay, m'lord," he says, "the king not be letting me go back. 'Stay here, Osbert,' he ordered. 'Ye've done yer duty.' And so here I stay. We be so worried about ye, m'lord."

Then he visibly gathers himself up. "Yer bath be ready, m'lord. And Sir Samuel be up here to bring me the salve for yer sores and tell me everything I be needing to know about how to dress yer sores and take care of yer feet."

He turns to Gwen. "His feet be going to smell of vinegar for a while, m'lady. I hope ye won't mind."

"His feet will be *here*, Osbert," she replies. "I care little what they smell like. Now let me settle Juliana for the night, and you take care of Alfred."

In my dressing room, Osbert helps me undress and get into a steaming bath.

"Sir Samuel say ye be excessive thin, m'lord, and so ye be. I be looking fer clothes that would fit, but mayhap they still be too big."

"We'll manage, Osbert. And see if you can find me some slippers, if you would. I've been told these feet will heal faster if I keep them out of my boots whenever I can. And with good food and your help to exercise, I'm sure I'll be back in my regular clothes in due course."

"Sir Samuel be telling me 'bout yer arm exercises, too. Ye can count on me to help, sir. I just be so happy ye be back with us."

When I walk back into our bed chamber, Gwen is standing before the fire in the lovely night dress she wore on our wedding night. I'm in awe once again of her beauty.

She takes one look at me with my night shirt hanging like giant's clothing on my thin frame, puts both hands to her cheeks in an overly dramatic gesture, and gasps, "My God, Alfred!" We both collapse on the couch in paroxysms of laughter.

I caress her cheek. "You're even more beautiful than I could remember over all those weeks." She nuzzles close to me. "It was thoughts of you and our child that got me through. Even when things were the darkest and I was near to despair, I knew I had to find a way to get back to you."

She kisses my face all over and whispers, "And somehow I knew in the depths of my being that you would come home. Even when some were near to giving up hope . . . "

She gently touches the skin near the sores on my wrists and neck, which I've left uncovered for the first time. "You're home now, Alfred. No one can do this to you anymore." She says no more, and her loving acceptance banishes all the anxiety I'd felt about her seeing me like this. She takes my hand and leads me to our bed, where she helps me in and pulls up the covers. "It's warmer here." Then she walks to the other side and climbs into bed beside me.

I turn to her and kiss her passionately, a passion she returns. "Gwen . . . my love . . . there's nothing I'd like more . . . but I don't think I have the strength yet."

"Even if you did," she whispers, "I'd have to ask you to wait another week. That whole business about being churched . . . I think it's ridiculous nonsense. I'll endure it for your grandfather's sake and public opinion. But the midwife says I need a full six weeks to heal from the birth. So we'll recover together. Right now, what I want most is for your face to be the last thing I see before I fall asleep and the first thing I see when I wake in the morning."

I kiss her again and she cuddles close. I am a very, very lucky man.

I'm vaguely aware of Gwen trying not to disturb me as she rises to start her day. I eventually wake to the sounds of Osbert moving about, opening the draperies to let in the morning light. When he observes me stirring he says, "I be told ye've become quite fond of porridge of a morning, sir. There be a fresh hot bowl of it ready fer ye here."

"Well, Osbert," I reply, "I'm not sure 'fond' is the word I'd have used; but as it seems to be helping me get my strength back, I suppose I should continue eating it for a while. You wouldn't perchance be able to rummage up some honey to pour on top of it, would you?"

"I have already, sir. That be the way I like me own porridge. And I find ye some slippers, too."

"I don't know how you do it, Osbert. I'm just grateful you do it for me."

An hour later, fed, dressed, pickled, and salved, I knock on the door of my grandfather's library. "Come." His voice is stronger than I'd expected.

I walk through the door to find him standing beside the fireplace, and he turns to watch as I cross the room. He still looks much older than when I last saw him, but there seems to be a brighter light in his eyes than even yesterday.

"If you're expecting your 'personal greeting' from me, Alfred, then I'm afraid you're just going to have to be disappointed."

I chuckle.

"I insisted they tell me about the dreadful state you were in when you showed up at the monastery. Looking at you now, I'm amazed how far you've come in just two weeks."

He looks carefully at my wrists and neck. I hold out one hand to allow him a better view. "Much progress indeed," he says, releasing my hand. "Now sit here and tell me everything." When we're seated, he adds, "And don't think for even a moment of sparing an old man any of the details. What you experienced cannot possibly be as horrible as what I've been imagining."

"You know me too well, Grandfather."

"First tell me . . . who was it that captured you? Who did this to you and why?"

"He called himself Ralf . . . said he was the third son of Ranulf. And he left no doubt as to his motives. I'll never forget what he said — 'You took my father from me, now I've taken you from your father.' Somehow he seemed to know that you and I have a special bond — he knew who I was without my telling him and kept referring to me as your favorite."

"Well," says my grandfather, "I'd be a foolish king indeed if I thought those who would wish to do me or our people harm didn't have eyes and ears among us. Now start at the beginning."

And so I tell him my story. He listens in silence, his face completely implacable, his composure never broken. I omit only one thing — the fact that I almost gave up one day too soon. He'll know how close I came to complete despair; there's no need to say that the story might easily have ended so very differently. I end by saying, "He's still out there somewhere, sir. I've no idea where."

When I finish we both watch the fire in silence for a long time. Finally he says, "I'm told that you insisted on keeping one of your shackles. May I see it?"

I hadn't known why I felt compelled to put it in my pocket as I was leaving our bed chamber, but now I'm glad I did. I pull it out and hand it to him. He turns it over and over, examining it from all sides, and then hands it back to me.

"There are not many men, Alfred, who'd have had the strength of mind to keep that. I think perhaps I'm not surprised that you did. You'll never regret that decision."

"Sir, may I ask . . . what became of Ronan Grai?"

"A fitting question indeed," he replies. "And one that has a very happy answer, I'm pleased to say. He and his squire survived the raid and were not taken as prisoners—thanks to you, Harold tells me. His knight's honor has been fully restored, and he's taken over as head of training. I believe he's going to be the best ever to hold that post since Cedric relinquished it."

"That's wonderful news. And I've no doubt he'll be a fine trainer."

"You should know," adds my grandfather, "that he also received a private commendation from me for his role in that affair."

"You know, sir, I've spent many hours trying to work it all out. Sir Ronan's insubordination and dismissal . . . then the message . . . then the raid. But I've not been able to fit all the pieces of the puzzle together."

"I rather expected you'd say that. And you have a right to know the truth of what led to your ordeal. That truth, however, lives inside something much bigger. I can tell you enough to make sense out of your ordeal without revealing the larger picture, but I think it's the right time for you to know more. It's your decision, of course."

I'm silent for a moment, contemplating what I may be walking into. But I told Gwen during our courtship that I wanted a meaningful role. Perhaps this is that opportunity. "I accept your judgment, Grandfather; you've never steered me wrong."

He rings a bell and his squire appears in the doorway. "Have some food and wine brought up for us, and ask Lord Rupert to join us, please."

Rupert arrives before the food. "Alfred, my boy. I'm told there's a very special greeting I'm to use for you now." He grins.

"Spare me, Uncle," I say laughingly.

"Actually, you look quite remarkable for someone who was as close to starvation as I've heard. And I quite like the beard!" Rupert has always had a short, closely trimmed beard himself.

"Not sure if I'll keep it, but I was advised not to try to shave until I get a bit healthier. Somehow I think Gwen may have the last word on that topic."

Over food and wine in front of the fire, Grandfather resumes. "You know the story of Ranulf's oath of vengeance, of course."

"Everyone does," I reply.

"Well, I think it's time for you to know what everyone else doesn't know. I'd heard the stories of the oath, of course, but paid them little mind. Men often say things in the heat of the moment that they later regret or back away from. It's true he deserted his duty, but he certainly wasn't the first man to do so nor would he be the last. The raids on the remote farms were worrisome, to be sure, but I was confident that a patrol would eventually be close enough by to catch them and bring them to justice.

"When Cedric was attacked, though, I had to face the fact that Ranulf posed a very real threat. They surely knew that we'd be on the hunt for them, and despite the fact that I ordered the patrols doubled, we couldn't find hide nor hair of them. Some months later, we got wind that they'd moved their operations to the Kingdom of Lakes. I'll admit it was tempting to let them be someone else's problem; but the Lakes kingdom has been our strongest ally for generations and their king is my great friend. I decided then and there that they were our problem to solve. We'd created them; we had to put an end to their mayhem. That's when I turned to my spymaster."

Rupert picks up the story. "I already had agents who could come and go in the Lakes . . . "

"Wait a minute," I interrupt him. "I thought your job was Ports and Tariffs Commissioner."

"That, too," he replies. "Think about it, Alfred. The port is full of all manner of men coming and going from the four corners of the earth, so my agents just blend into the landscape. We also hear things from those who have routine business there . . . ship captains, traders, wagoners bringing trade goods to the dock. And what *we* don't hear, the tavern-keepers and brothel owners do. It's the best place imaginable as a base of operations."

"I'm . . . I'm at a loss for words."

"Of course, he," Rupert nods toward his father, "insists I actually collect the tariffs, too, so it's not entirely fun and games."

"But you have to admit it works well that way," Grandfather chuckles as Rupert grins.

"Anyway," Rupert continues, "we were able to track them easily in the Lakes and managed to disrupt most of their plots. We were so successful, in fact, that they finally went to ground for many years up in the far northern reaches of the Lakes. I was actually hopeful that we'd put an end to their mischief once and for all. But then we heard from Elvin that they'd gone to the Peaks."

"I remember his telling us about that when I went on the trade mission." I pause for a moment. "Wait a minute, Uncle . . . is Elvin one of your agents?"

Rupert grins at his father once again. "I told you he'd figure things out quickly." My uncle's sense of humor is both the boon and the bane of our family interactions. "More of a conduit," he resumes seriously. "As the king's stable master, Elvin can't easily move about the kingdom without being recognized. On the other hand, people tell him things they might not say to others, and he can get messages to us from other agents without their having to leave their posts.

"But having Ranulf and his gang in the Peaks made things harder, especially since they were using the highlands as their base. The people up there are very clannish and suspicious of strangers, so getting an agent in is next to impossible. I'm still not sure why they seemed to accept Ranulf. They certainly weren't eager to take his bait that they should join him to attack the lowlanders; but then they have long memories up there and wouldn't have forgotten that the mother of their king was a highlander herself—the daughter of a clan chief. In any event, Elvin became convinced Ranulf was back to his old ways, with revenge on us being his ultimate goal."

"We'll never know for sure," says Grandfather, "why he decided to come back, but I've often wondered if it was the pressure of time. Ranulf's a couple of years older than Cedric and me, so if he truly felt honor-bound by that oath, he might have been worried his time was running out.

"In any event, Elvin's suspicions turned out to be right. You were there in the Council meeting, Alfred, when their threat to our trade expeditions was discussed. We had no choice but to strengthen the protection for those missions. To do otherwise would've played into Ranulf's hand and put our alliance with the Peaks at risk. But that left me with a different dilemma. If we succeeded in thwarting him in the Peaks, where would they go then?"

"*My* guess," Rupert picks up the story, "was that they'd head for the Territories . . . probably overland where the lowlands of the Peaks border the far Western Territories. And then, they'd have been out of our reach. It would've been almost impossible for me to get anyone into that part of the world. If you weren't born on some lord's lands, then you're a stranger there by definition. I might have been able to use traveling tradesmen or craftsmen, but they couldn't linger anywhere, so what they could learn would be limited. And it's a long and dangerous route home if they found themselves in trouble. I especially didn't like the prospect of someone being caught and their real purpose exposed."

"It was my decision not to take that risk," Grandfather again. "But that meant we had to come up with something else that would tempt them. The reservoir project seemed just the thing. Close enough to the Peaks that Ranulf would be confident of an easy escape route, but within our borders so that it would be undeniable that their crime had been committed on our soil. Harold's presence there could serve as a temptation, but we couldn't just wait around and hope they saw the opportunity for themselves. We had to lure them into the attack, but it had to be done with the utmost stealth so that Ranulf wouldn't suspect a trap. Rupert devised the plan."

"Sir Ronan," Rupert now, "was on the verge of retirement and willing to take on a final assignment for the king, even though it meant enduring public dishonor and the risk of death either at Ranulf's hands or in the skirmish. So we spun the web. The fact that he was a good engineer meant that Harold wouldn't question the assignment. We made up the bits about his thwarted aspirations to be knight commander and his tendency to fractiousness as a result. Ronan was only too happy to go along. It was his father, you see, who was killed when Cedric was attacked."

"So Uncle Harold knew none of this?" I ask. "You asked me not to reveal my role, but he knew *nothing* of what was afoot?"

"That, too, was my decision." Grandfather. "What I told Harold was that Ronan was on the verge of being dismissed for his fractiousness and that I'd intervened because I knew Harold needed another engineer. But I made it perfectly clear that any failure of discipline should be dealt with swiftly and harshly, since I had no intention that the king's generosity be abused. I felt a certain amount of guilt about keeping Harold in the dark, but for our plan to work, Ronan's dismissal had to be completely natural and Harold's anger unquestionable. There was no way to know whose eyes and ears might be lurking among the people working on the project."

"Despite the fact that the troops at Harold's disposal should have been able to deal with four men," Rupert, "we wanted to have reinforcements on hand in case something went wrong. But if we sent them in advance, that sort of disruption to the normal routine of the camp would be suspicious. That's why we needed the information about when the attack was planned. What we couldn't know until the last minute was when the attack would be or that Ranulf had more than doubled the size of his gang. But it was a risk we had to take. The other thing we couldn't possibly have known was that Captain Arnald and half the troops would be off pursuing the perceived threat. You have to admire Ranulf's strategy of drawing them away.

"The knight commander led the reinforcements himself and really drove his men. Some of them told me they rode so hard, they were afraid of pushing their horses to exhaustion. They arrived in time to quash the attack, but not in time to save you."

"So you see, Alfred," says my grandfather, "it was a plot that worked so very well on the one hand but with such terrible consequences on the other. Ranulf is dead, and we brought two of his sons to justice. But at such a terrible cost to you. And with one loose end still not resolved. It's part of the burden that comes with the crown – and a guilt I will bear for the rest of my life."

"I blame no one, Grandfather."

"That's easy to say now that you're safely home."

"But I don't say it lightly. I spent hours talking about my ordeal with Lord and Lady Ernle and with Samuel on the ride home. That helped me really grasp that it was all over and come to grips with the fact that sometimes life doesn't give us what we expected. I refuse to accept the priests' view that it was all God's plan, but it gives me a great deal of comfort to fully understand why it happened. I thank you for that."

"It's not easy to keep a kingdom safe, Alfred. I've been fortunate beyond measure to have Rupert by my side. But his role is a closely guarded secret and must remain so. You're now one of the very few privileged to know it."

"I'd never betray your trust, Grandfather."

"You've already proven that. Harold told me he knew nothing of the message you sent me or of the imminent raid. He's also convinced that your inviting him to drink and rest the night with you is what saved his life.

"What I want you to consider doing now is to help Rupert help me protect the kingdom. I'm not suggesting you be directly involved in managing agents or spying on your own. What we need is another good mind to help work out what the threats may be and how to deal with them. We both think you're the best we have to do that."

We sit in silence for a very long time. This is a lot to take in. In the end, the only thing I can find to say is, "I'm humbled . . . honored . . . I'll do my very best."

"There's one more thing, Alfred," says my grandfather, switching from his serious tone to something more light-hearted. "In two weeks' time, I intend to have a celebration to honor the returning hero. I've ordered preparations for a huge banquet here and for food, drink, and celebration in the town for the people."

"Sir, I'm no hero . . . just a survivor."

"You're a hero in the people's eyes, Alfred, and we should allow them to celebrate that. Every man who knows of your plight is now asking himself if he had been your shoes, would he have had the strength to make it through. Most of them will likely think they would not, so your survival and return make you a hero to them."

"One thing I've learned," I say. "Men have inner strength that they don't even know is there until fate forces them to find it. I only hope that most men are never faced with the need."

In the coming two weeks, I settle back into my life. I'm regaining weight and strength. I can now lift my arms enough to mount Star Dancer with only a leg up from the groom. The sores on my wrists and neck are completely healed, though the slight scars will always remind me of that dreadful time. And I'm starting to see some normal color at the base of my toe nails.

I've come to know and love my baby daughter in a way I could never have imagined. Gwen is as perfect a mother as she has always been a wife.

I've not yet been told what the king has in mind for me next. That, he says, will wait until he's satisfied I've fully recovered.

Preparations for the celebration proceed apace. The hunting parties have returned and the kitchens are running all day and night. The guests are beginning to arrive, including Gwen's parents who came early to spend time with their new granddaughter.

The king has ordered that I be seated on his right, in the place of highest honor, with Gwen by my side. We'll use the banquet as an opportunity to introduce the world to our Juliana.

When I learned of it, I asked my grandfather, somewhat to his surprise, if we might suspend normal protocol entirely for the banquet. He raised his eyebrows as he asked, "What did you have in mind?"

"Well, sir, you said this celebration is for the people, so I'd like to make it just that and honor the people who gave me back my life. If you'd agree, sir, I'd like to have Fulk the blacksmith seated to your left, the infirmerer beside him, and then Prior André. Lord Ernle would be beside Gwen along with his squire, Thomas, and Samuel. The rest of the seating arrangements can be worked out by those who know how best to do it."

My grandfather beamed with delight. "Alfred," he clapped me on the shoulder, "it's brilliant . . . and frankly, I'm ashamed I didn't think of it myself."

The banquet is a huge success. Fulk is beside himself with glee at getting to sit next to the king. During the afternoon, my grandfather had spent quite some time alone with Prior André, talking of their old friend Francis. This seems to have brought him some measure of closure, for he appears even more content this evening than I've seen him since my return. We learn that André is to take up Francis's position as abbot, the monks having unanimously voted to request his return. No doubt this is additional comfort for my grandfather.

Just after the main course, Gwen excuses herself to feed Juliana and then leaves the baby in Nurse's care for the remainder of the evening, most of which is given over to dancing. When Gwen invites Fulk to partner her, he looks as if he might quite literally burst with delight. Later, when she and I are dancing together, she whispers in my ear, "Do you think tonight might be a good time to make a start on a brother for Juliana?" She has a knack for saying or doing the most provocative things when I least expect them . . . and this time it takes all my self-control to suppress a physical reaction that might be obvious if anyone were paying attention. All I can do is savor the notion of what awaits me when it's finally seemly for us to make our way upstairs.

My grandfather retires early so that the celebrating can continue without the need for formal protocol. Though I know he's enjoyed this evening, he tires more easily than I've ever seen, reminding me once again that his days are numbered. As I watch him make his way slowly out of the hall, the thought comes to me unbidden: what will our lives ever be like without him?

Author's Notes

Many authors of historical fiction choose to eschew the use of contractions in favor of more formal dialogue and narrative. That is a stylistic choice that each author must make for themselves. In fact, many people believe that written and spoken language in medieval and Renaissance times was more stilted and formal than it is today.

A bit of research, however, reveals that contractions, in the English language at least, have been with us for many centuries. Even as far back as Old English, *nis* was the contraction of *ne is*, which means "is not." Similarly, *naefde* came from *ne haefde*, or "did not have." Middle English also had its contractions: *thilke* for *the ilke* ("the same"), *noot* for *ne woot* ("knows not"), or *nere* for *ne were* ("were not"). Because punctuation had not yet developed, there are no visual clues in written texts that these words are contractions. It was merely understood by the reader or speaker.

By Shakespeare's time, contractions were widespread. The Bard used them profusely in his plays—often, of course, to get the meter right. But one must assume they were well known at the time, else how would playgoers have understood what was being said on stage?

It's on this basis that I've made the decision to use contractions liberally in both the narrative and dialogue within this series. I find it provides a more natural flow and allows my readers to more easily identify with the characters and feel a deeper sense of immersion in the story. To avoid driving them crazy, though, I've used the modern forms, complete with apostrophes ☺.

I've tried to be diligent about avoiding linguistic anachronisms (well, anachronisms in general), such as references to someone "going off half-cocked" before guns were even invented. In some cases, however, I've made the conscious choice to use a more modern word to preclude my readers' having to scurry to the dictionary over and over (or worse yet, give up on the book altogether). Use of the word "wagon" is an example of such a choice. In Alfred's time, people would have used "wain" to refer to such a conveyance; but since "wagon" came into common usage in the mid-1500s, I've opted to make the reader's life easier by using the more recognizable word. On the other hand, I've explicitly chosen to use some period-appropriate words—particularly slang—for authenticity and for "flavor." Wherever I've made such a choice, I don't think the reader will have much difficulty working out the meaning. Names of characters (both forenames and surnames) are all authentic for the period.

The tinderbox that Alfred carries on his first encampment (and will use many times later in his life) is a slight stretch for the period. Flint and fire steel had been in use since the Iron Age to produce sparks for starting a fire. The Wikipedia article on fire steel states:

"From the Iron Age forward, until the invention of the friction match, the use of flint and steel was a common method of firelighting [sic]. Percussion fire-starting was prevalent in Europe during ancient times, the Middle Ages and the Viking Age.

"When flint and steel were used, the fire steel was often kept in a metal tinderbox together with flint and tinder."

But the earliest citation of the word tinderbox given by the Oxford English Dictionary is 1530. I've chosen to make things easy for Alfred by allowing him a container for his flint and fire steel and giving it a name (tinderbox) that should be readily understood by the modern reader.

Another topic that we're often tempted to think of as a modern invention, given that protecting our information on all our electronic gadgets has become a common concern these days, is encryption. The notion of coded messages is, however, a far older idea.

One of the earliest recorded uses of encryption techniques is the Caesar Cipher, so named because of its use by Julius Caesar to send secret messages during his military campaigns. It is a simple alphabetic substitution cipher in which the receiver need only know the sender's offset to decode the message. Julius Caesar was known to use an offset of three, meaning that the letter "D" would be substituted for "A" in the coded message.

Alphabetic substitution is something even children do at play when they randomly assign one letter to stand in for another and then write messages in code. The problem with this random approach is that both sender and receiver must be in possession of identical tables showing the assignments – and must take extraordinary measures to safeguard those tables lest they fall into the wrong hands. (This method is actually the basis for the one-time pads used in modern espionage, but that's a discussion for a different time and place.)

Caesar's simplification meant that sender and receiver could store the key in their heads, eliminating the additional risk of safeguarding code tables (perhaps not the easiest thing to do on a battlefield) or transmitting the key by a courier who could be waylaid and bribed or coerced into parting with the information. The substitution table could be constructed on the fly – when needed for encoding or decoding – and then destroyed, just as Alfred does when he needs to get Sir Ronan's message secretly to the king.

This novel is a work of fiction that tells the story of what might have been in a world that doesn't precisely correspond to the one we know. Readers will note similarities with northern Europe, but my decision to fictionalize the setting was a matter of practicality for my characters. European history from this period and its major actors are too well known for it to be plausible that a different set of kings and nobility might actually have existed. The fictional setting also gave me the freedom to embed the allegory of our own times within Alfred's story. *Second Son* deals with coming of age and taking a place on the world's stage. Subsequent volumes of the series will explore other issues.

For those who prefer to read the Second Son Chronicles solely as entertainment, I hope you get as much enjoyment from immersing yourself in Alfred's world as I've had in bringing his tale to life.

About the Author

Pamela Taylor brings her love of history to the art of story-telling for the first time. An avid reader of historical fact and fiction, she finds the past offers rich sources for character, ambiance, and plot that allow readers to escape into a world totally unlike their daily lives. She shares her home with two Corgis who remind her frequently that a dog walk is the best way to find inspiration for that next chapter.

View other Black Rose Writing titles at www.blackrosewriting.com/books and
use promo code **PRINT** to receive a **20% discount** when purchasing.

BLACK ROSE
writing™

9 781684 330638